DOLPHIN
FRIENDLY

DOLPHIN
FRIENDLY

•

Jessica Andersen

AVALON BOOKS
NEW YORK

PRINTED IN THE UNITED STATES OF AMERICA
ON ACID-FREE PAPER
BY HADDON CRAFTSMEN, BLOOMSBURG, PENNSYLVANIA

To my grandparents Ken and Marian Woodard,
with fond memories of summers on Cape Cod.

Chapter One

Maddy Jamison heard a muffled thud at the front of the Inn, as though someone had tripped on the granite steps and landed face-first on the freshly stained porch. There was a curse and a scuffling sound, and she abandoned her dusting—gee, that was a huge disappointment—to answer the summons.

She didn't pause as she passed the huge old mirror that her grandfather had shipped back from France after the war. She knew what she'd see—a woman who was a little too thin in some places, too plump in others, wearing a smudged T-shirt and jeans that were unfit to be seen in public but served just fine for a cleaning jag.

Her hair would be a mess. It always was. The

sticky, salty breeze that blew off Cape Cod Bay and through the open windows of the Smuggler's Inn was guaranteed to add body to the limpest curls, and the last thing Maddy's hair needed was more body.

In desperation that morning, she'd tied a blue scarf around the fluffy mass and cinched it tight, hoping that she could make it through her housework without giving in to impulse and having Bambi-with-an-"i" at the Clip-n-Curl just cut it all off.

She'd tried that once. Just once, right after she moved to Smuggler's Cove and started her life over. Her short hair had defied mousse and spray, insisting instead on standing straight up in pointy strawberry-blond spikes that made her look like a punk rocker. Or, as her friend Levi had commented, a pink sea urchin.

Leave it to Levi.

The thumping on the porch ceased as Maddy jogged down the front stairs, and she wondered whether it had been the mailman delivering a package, perhaps those chenille curtains she'd ordered for the back bedroom or the p-chem text she'd bought from an online bookstore. But Jerry would've let himself in the back door and dropped off the mail while angling for a cup of tea or a scone, just like any of her other friends in the little town.

As she hit the bottom step, the doorbell gave its trademark apoplectic gurgle, the one Levi always claimed sounded like a duck caught in a wine press. Maddy made a mental note to have someone look at the mechanism. Again.

Who could it be? Most of the door-to-door salesmen were kept at bay by the *Warning: Attack Cat* sign on the gate, and she had no guests scheduled to arrive for two more days.

She resolutely pushed aside thoughts of her incoming guests, and the niggling doubts she had about allowing them into her home, opened the front door—

And wished she had taken the time to look in the mirror.

In fact, she wished she had taken the time to run down to her private suite of rooms, shower, blow dry her hair until it took on some semblance of style, and dress herself in something improbably sexy—which, come to think of it, she didn't own.

Because unless her dust-crusted eyes betrayed her, the man leaning against the frame of the front door with his thumb on her quacking doorbell was the most perfect, most gorgeous thing she had seen in her entire life.

Oh, my, she thought. *Look what just washed up on the shores of Smuggler's Cove.* The sight of him boggled her so much she hardly noticed the beach reference, something she avoided when possible. But she was unable to avoid the odor that came off of him in waves. Or schools.

Fish.

She hated the smell of fish. It reminded her of . . . well, horrible things that she didn't want to be reminded of.

But otherwise, he might have stepped right out of one of the books she left in her bedroom instead of the downstairs library she kept for her guests. One of those books whose covers feature a heroine with perfect hair clinging to a half-naked warrior with an enormous sword.

"Excuse me?" His voice was deep, and rumbled through his chest as if each word was an effort. "Is this the Smuggler's Inn?"

His jet-black hair curled just enough to save the lean planes of his face from being too hard, and the dimple in his chin might have made him look boyish if it hadn't been offset by a jagged scar low on his stubbled jaw that stood out in stark relief to the warm, glowing bronze of his skin.

Give him a dagger and a parrot and she'd have herself a pirate, one who had stepped right out of the Legend of Smuggler's Cove. Or out of one of those novels where the seafaring brigand abducts the heroine with the nice hair and throws her in the brig until her love reforms him and they sail off into the sunset to raise their family on a little-known tropical island paradise.

Maddy liked stories like that except for the parts about being on the high seas, which she skipped over until the author got back to the good stuff.

The pirate on her porch was tall, rangy, and he stood like a sailor, with muscled legs spread as if to provide balance on a swaying deck. His booted feet rested one step down from her, but still she had to tilt her head up a notch to look him in the eyes.

Eyes that watched her steadily though they were glazed with fatigue as he sagged against the side of her house. Eyes the fathomless blue-green of a rogue wave off the Great Barrier Reef.

Eyes that reminded her of her dreams. And her nightmares.

Enough, she thought with a stern mental shake. *Get a hold of yourself, Madelyne. He's just a man.* She wiped a suddenly sweaty palm on her jeans before offering it to him with a smile that felt dusty and unkempt, just like her.

"Yes, this is the Smuggler's Inn. I'm Maddy Jamison, the owner. Can I help you? If you're looking for a room, I'm afraid I can only keep you for one night."

Her face heated at how that had come out, but he didn't seem to notice when he pushed himself away from the door frame, swaying slightly as he gripped her hand and smiled in return.

Electricity zinged its way up her arm at the touch of his hand on hers and the smell of fish suddenly intensified, swirling around her in a finny rush that had her gasping and stepping back into the safety of the house. The brain cells that hadn't drained to her toes at his appearance spluttered back to life and she had a sudden unnerving thought. What if this was one of the guests whose arrival she was dreading?

He was still smiling and laugh lines crinkled at the corners of his tired blue-green eyes, drawing attention to dark lashes that would have done a mascara model proud. "Thank goodness. I know I'm a few days early, but can I have a room anyway? I'm Brody Davenport."

The faint twang in his husky voice brought to mind safe images of cows and endless fields, but the smell of fish stirred ripples of memory.

Disappointment quashed the quick thrill Davenport's good looks had brought, and suddenly Maddy didn't mind so much that she'd answered the door looking like . . . well, like herself. Because there was only one thing she disliked more than the smell of fish and the sight of the ocean. One thing she distrusted more than the nauseating sway of boats and the greasy feel of salt water on her skin.

There was one thing, or rather one group of people she blamed for her empty childhood, lack of a graduate degree, and pretty much everything that had gone wrong in her life before or since—a group of rootless, irresponsible people that Maddy had no love for.

Marine biologists. Like her parents. Like her incoming guests, the members of Dolphin Friendly. And especially like their leader, Brody Davenport.

He wasn't a pirate bent upon a romantic kidnapping. She could have forgiven him that. He wasn't a rogue Scot looking to marry an enemy's daughter, or a warrior pillaging his way across medieval Europe. She could have forgiven him those things as well.

No, he was a marine biologist. And she would never forgive him that.

Brody saw the woman's smile slip, saw the interest fade in her stormy blue eyes, and would have taken the time to wonder at the sudden change—but he was almost dead on his feet.

In fact, death was starting to look better and better. If he was dead, or at least in a coma or something, he'd be lying down for a very, very long time, right? Because he was dead tired, and it was all Smitty's fault. Somehow, it had to be Smitty's fault.

Brody and the other members of Dolphin Friendly had been planning the Smuggler's Cove Project for months now, and for once they had everything ready to go on schedule—but of course something happened at the last minute to foul up the timetable.

As usual.

It wasn't like he could have ignored the call and gone on with his packing. Forty white-sided dolphins and a couple of bottlenose stranded off Provincetown needed his help and he wasn't about to say, "Sorry guys, can't help you today, but if you'd like to beach yourselves in Smuggler's Cove a week or so from now, I'll be happy to fit you in."

Nope, couldn't say that. So he'd dumped the rest of the prep work on his so-called assistant, Smitty, and hightailed it out to P'town where he and a handful of other stranding rescue volunteers spent a filthy, cold twenty hours in and out of the water trying to save a pod that didn't want to be saved.

They'd refloated one out of forty-three, and the odds were that the enormous bottlenose female with the scarred dorsal fin would just end up beached further down the coast. Once stranding was on a dolphin's mind, there wasn't much a two-legged land dweller could do to change it— and the more human beings mucked with the dolphin's natural habitat, the more common such strandings became.

Discouraged, smelly, and incredibly tired, Brody had hitched a ride back to the local rescue center and showered there, thankful that his rucksack contained a change of clothing. On his way out, he'd stopped to have a peek at the animal care center, where almost thirty harbor seal pups stranded in the late winter and early spring had been treated and fattened up, and were almost ready for release back into the wild.

It was moments like those that made stranding rescue worthwhile. When he watched the fat gray seal pups tumble over one another, glowing with health and vigor—a far cry from the skinny waifs that had been brought in by Dolphin Friendly and others like them—Brody felt a warm glow in his chest and couldn't help smiling.

He was still smiling when he'd headed through the kitchens and waved to a few friends as they prepared the pups' final meal of the day.

Then disaster struck.

He'd almost made it safely out the door when one of the volunteers put an enormous chunk of frozen mackerel down the industrial garbage disposal, which backed up violently in protest. The resulting geyser had erupted with a flourish, painting the entire kitchen and its inhabitants with pureed fish.

The others had screamed and run for cover. Brody just stood by the door and dripped.

So much for his clean clothes.

He was too annoyed to stop and buy new duds, too tired to drive back up north to where Dolphin Friendly was bivouacked. He thought about napping in the Jeep, but five minutes in the warm car was enough for the smell to make his eyes water. Then he thought of the Smuggler's Inn.

Sure, their reservations didn't start for another day or so, but he was positive he could talk his way into a room. Best of all, he remembered that the brochure had boasted a laundry service.

He'd driven to Smuggler's Cove, Cape Cod in a haze of exhaustion, his vision graying as he struggled to read the directions Smitty had scrawled on the back of a Cap'n Crunch box as Brody had been running out the door to the stranding.

The resort town was a blur, the house big and white, the doorbell odd, and the woman prettier than pretty. But neither tourist attractions nor pretty women were high on his list of priorities— the only things he cared about at that moment were a shower, a bed, and clean clothes. In that order.

So he stumbled into the Inn, past his startled hostess and into a nicely carpeted hallway. He dropped the rucksack that contained his stinking stranding clothes right on a spotless Oriental runner, slung his shortie wetsuit over his shoulder—he wasn't sure why he was carrying it and couldn't be bothered to put it back in the Jeep—and staggered halfway up the stairs before he remembered that he didn't have a room.

"I know I'm early. Can I have a bed anyway?" She looked dubious and for a moment Brody considered getting on his knees and begging, but he didn't think he could have gotten back up afterward and didn't fancy sleeping in the hallway. So he tried his most beseeching look, the one that usually got him whatever he wanted, and said, "Please?"

After what seemed like an eternity, she nodded slowly and pointed at the second door on the right.

He staggered the rest of the way up the stairs, calling over his shoulder, "Thanks. I'll leave my clothes out in the hall for the laundry people. Make sure they don't shrink anything." And practically fell into his room.

Misjudging the distance, he slammed the door hard enough to rattle the mirror and almost collapsed onto the bed, fishy clothes and all.

"Not yet," he muttered, regaining his equilibrium with almost superhuman effort. "Shower first."

He stripped, shuddering at the feel of sticky

cloth separating from his skin, and shoved the stinking bundle into the hall, closing the door more gently this time. Hopefully the laundry service would be able to do something with it, because otherwise he was out of luck until Smitty, Violet, and the others arrived.

Naked, he padded to the bathroom and opened the door. It was a closet.

He tried the other door. A Murphy bed.

"Where is the bathroom?" He hadn't meant to shout, but it had been that kind of day. It was just bad luck his hostess was outside the room, presumably gathering up his laundry, and heard his outburst.

Her soft voice mildly reproving, she said through the door, "The bathroom is at the end of the hall, Mr. Davenport. Only one of our rooms has a private bath and it was reserved for a Mr. Smith."

Trust Smitty to snag the best room. Brody snarled—quietly—and made a mental note to do the reservations himself the next time they decided to have a land-based operation. Too late, he heard footsteps as Maddy Jamison headed back down the stairs with his clothes. All of them.

His day just kept getting better and better.

* * *

Maddy was fuming as she stomped downstairs. Absolutely fuming. Who did this Davenport guy think he was, staggering through her home like a drunk, ordering her around as if she was his servant, then complaining about the room she'd let him have two whole days early?

Besides, being angry was far easier than thinking about who he was. What he was.

And what he wasn't.

A few tendrils of hair escaped the control of her kerchief and slithered across her cheek as she stared at the bundle in her arms. The skin on her arms prickled as the light from her grandmother's stained glass chandelier glinted off the fish scales that dotted Davenport's clothing.

He actually expected her to wash this stuff? She'd rather burn it.

Enjoying that image, she started to carry the filthy garments to the laundry room, then remembered she'd left the detergent upstairs after hand washing the lace curtains in the guest bathroom as part of her interrupted cleaning fit.

Thinking back over those first few moments of interruption, when she'd had the freedom to imagine that the man at the door had stepped out of her fantasies rather than her nightmares, Maddy allowed herself a brief spurt of self-pity before quashing it ruthlessly and grinding it beneath her mental heel.

She'd never been lucky in that sort of thing before, why should today be any different?

Irritably, she jabbed a handful of hair back into the kerchief and was heading back upstairs to retrieve the soap—or the lighter fluid, whichever came to hand first—when she was interrupted by a noise from Davenport's room.

Was he planning on yelling at her through the door again? He'd better not, if he knew what was good for him.

But no, he was headed for the shower, apparently unaware of her presence. His door opened and closed quietly and she was struck nearly dumb when her newest guest sauntered down the hall toward the bath.

Wearing a wetsuit.

"He was wearing *what?*" Chrissy muffled a giggle behind her hand and leaned as far across the washing machine as she could, considering she was five months pregnant. "You're kidding."

Maddy shook her head and fought a grin as she dumped Davenport's pants into the washing machine. "Nope. It was almost as strange as the time I caught that seventy-year-old couple in the vacuum closet jousting with the feather dusters."

Christine wrinkled her pert nose and waved the image away. "Please, I'd prefer to picture Davenport in a shortie wetsuit. He looked pretty good from across the boardwalk when he knocked on your door. How is he up close?"

Maddy repressed the urge to ask whether her friend wanted the with- or without-wetsuit opinion. The truth was, Brody Davenport looked entirely too good in either situation for her peace of mind.

"He's . . ." She trailed off, trying to describe him accurately. Dark? Dangerous? Magnetic? Compelling? All understatements. Chrissy leaned forward expectantly, and Maddy finally expelled a breath and finished with a lame, "Okay."

The other woman snorted. "Okay? That's pretty weak even for you, Madelyne."

Maddy winced. When Chrissy used her given name it was a sure sign she knew something was up. "He's handsome, okay? Gorgeous. Practically a statue. And he's one of *them.*"

"One of . . ." Chrissy winced. "Oh. I'm sorry, Maddy. I wasn't thinking. I'd forgotten the marine biologists were coming, really I had." She shook her hair away from her face and laid a gentle hand on her friend's shoulder. "Why'd you take the reservation if you knew it was going to bother you?"

"The money," Maddy answered with a casual shrug that she hoped camouflaged the importance of her next words. "I want to go back to school."

It had been nine years since she'd left grad school with her doctorate unfinished. Nine years since she'd come back to Smuggler's Cove to take over for her grandparents when they conveniently "retired" to Florida. Nine years since her parents died.

Nine years of drifting through life, of running the Inn because it was simpler than doing something else, of dating Kevin because he was easy and undemanding. Comfortable.

When had comfortable stopped being enough? Maddy wasn't sure, but somehow over the last couple of years she had stopped accepting the easy way and started to remember a child who had rebelled against the simple things and demanded a challenge. Demanded danger. Excitement.

Longed to be a part of things.

She might not be that child anymore, but she had broken things off with Kevin just the same. And now she wanted to go back to school. Take a venture into the unknown. And she was afraid of what her friends would think. They had been shocked by the end of her engagement to the head chef at Mary Jo's, and Maddy feared that another big change would just stir things up again. She'd been the focus of gossip back when she moved to Smuggler's Cove, and she didn't care to repeat the experience.

But bless her, Chrissy's reaction was instantaneous and wholehearted support. "Maddy! That's wonderful!"

Maddy laughed a little in relief as her friend grabbed her arms and swung her in a little dance while some of Davenport's smelly clothes slid off the washing machine and landed on the floor with a disgusting plop.

"I've always thought there was more out there for you than this—not that there's anything wrong with running your grandparents' Inn, of course. I'm just not sure it's enough," Chrissy babbled, as was her habit when she was excited. "Where will you go? Are you leaving us? What are you going to study?"

Maddy didn't have an answer for that. In fact, she'd surprised herself. Once the words were said out loud, they seemed far scarier than they had just rattling around in her brain.

She was going back to school. She was going to pick up her life where it had all but ended nine years ago. What was she going to study? Who would she be when she was done? She shook her head and felt the kerchief slide perilously atop her head.

Maybe she'd celebrate the decision with another attempt at a short hairdo. It couldn't be any worse than the last one, which had taken almost three years to grow out past a hideous finger-in-the-electric-socket halo.

"I don't know," she said. "I'm just thinking about going back to school, you know? Anyway, even with financial aid it'll take more money than I have, and the opportunity to book the whole place full for three weeks during the spring slowdown is too good to pass up. So marine biologists it is, whether I like it or not. If I'm lucky, they'll be too busy to spend any time at home."

Her parents always had been.

"And besides," Chrissy said, "what these guys do really has no bearing on what happened back then. It's like comparing apples to oranges. They're both round fruit, but the similarity stops there."

Or like comparing haddock to tuna, Maddy thought. *When you come right down to it, they're both fish.*

Mood slowly deflating, she concentrated on shoving more of Davenport's scaly, smelly clothing into the machine, leaving the rest of it on the floor where it belonged.

She toggled the water to hot, not really caring if the stuff shrank or not, and added three cups of extra-strength gardenia-scented detergent—the kind she used for cleaning her braided rugs. As an afterthought, she added a slug of lavender stain remover and deodorizer.

She considered throwing in a gallon of bleach and decided that would be overkill. Cranking the whole mess to ON, she slammed the lid and hit the button that would eradicate that horrible smell from her house.

"So when do we get to meet the newest inhabitant of Smuggler's Cove?" Chrissy asked with a glint in her eye.

Refusing to be drawn back into a conversation about Davenport, Maddy stopped herself from glancing up to the second floor where he slept. "I'm not sure. He took a shower and crashed in his room. I haven't heard a peep since. I'll knock at dinnertime, but I'd be surprised to see his face before tomorrow."

"I don't suppose we could take a look, just to make sure he's okay?" Chrissy's voice was hopeful and Maddy had to laugh.

"Shame on you. You're a married woman, remember?"

Chrissy shrugged. "You're not."

No, she wasn't. Maddy suffered a quick spasm of regret for her broken engagement. She'd like to be married now and expecting a child like Chrissy was, would like to be loved and cherished and fussed over, like Kevin had tried to do.

But, she consoled herself, one day she would meet a man who could give her all those things, along with a healthy dose of the excitement and intellectual challenge that had been sadly lacking in her relationship with Kev.

This fantasy husband would be solid and kind, dependable and dashing—he'd be an accountant or a truck driver, a rodeo clown or a farmer, a lawyer or a doctor—her own personal hero who kept his feet firmly planted on dirt and pavement and wouldn't question the fact that she lived in a seaside resort town and never went down by the ocean.

As Chrissy let herself out, Maddy thought she heard a noise from the second floor and looked again in Davenport's direction, reliving the sight of him parading down the upstairs hall in a wetsuit.

She would find a man of the land, and have her children with him, she told herself firmly. No matter how handsome he might be, she would never be interested in an itinerant, waterlogged researcher with no need for solid ground and no understanding of family or responsibility or real life.

She *couldn't* be interested, because she'd vowed long ago never to love a man like her father.

Chapter Two

Early the next morning, Brody floundered his way out of sleep and discovered that somebody had snuck into his berth and jammed a pair of old sweatsocks in his mouth while he slept.

Again.

He hated it when Smitty did stuff like that, so he groaned around the socks and rolled over in his hammock.

And fell out of bed.

Brody yelped when the back of his head rapped against the floor. Flopping about like a landed harbor porpoise in an attempt to regain legs that weren't quite awake yet, he wound up face-down on a braided rug that smelled faintly of flowers and was warm from the yellow sun that slanted between lace curtains. He paused.

Braided rug. Lace. Sunlight.

No berth. No hammock. Thankfully, no sweatsocks. He wasn't even in the cramped living quarters of his beloved *Streaker*. He was on land, in a room at the Smuggler's Inn.

And boy, did he need a toothbrush.

And some clothes.

He dimly recalled staggering into the place the day before, thought he remembered an angel meeting him at the door and spiriting his laundry away. He wondered if it had come back yet. The laundry, not the angel.

Levering himself up, Brody winced as his body protested the motion with a thousand tiny screams of pain.

Once upon a time, he could have worked a huge stranding for two days in a row and gone out dancing afterward, maybe chatted up a pretty girl to help him forget the sight of a whole pod drowning in fresh air. These days, he was lucky if he could tie his own shoes the next day, never mind flirt.

He'd never thought of thirty-three as old before.

Groaning, he pulled himself to his feet and shivered a little as a tricky sea breeze wandered its way between the curtains and feathered across his chest. Unaccountably the sensation brought to mind the image of the angel with the laundry, and he paused and cocked his head. Was she really as pretty as he remembered?

He shrugged and laughed at himself. As tired as he'd been the night before, the hostess at the Smuggler's Inn could've been ninety years old and bucktoothed and he would have thought her beautiful as long as she gave him a bed and cleaned his clothes.

Speaking of which . . . Brody looked toward the door and there they were, cleaned and folded just inside his room. He grinned and pulled on his jeans and shirt before opening the door that he thought ought to lead to the hall.

Either that, or to the Murphy bed.

The door led to the hall, which was filled with the welcome smell of eggs, toast, and . . .

"Coffee," he breathed like a prayer. Coffee that Smitty hadn't made, coffee that didn't taste like it was half bilge water.

Real coffee. Heaven. Every cell of his body cried out for it, and in his haste to find that magical liquid, Brody leaped straight out of the room—

And tripped over his landlady, who absolutely, positively was neither ninety years old nor bucktoothed.

She squeaked in surprise and fell back on her rear while Brody performed a complicated tap dance to avoid trampling her, all the while trying not to stare.

She was lovely, classic, elegant, refined—all those things he rarely appreciated when he was looking for a quick *Hey, I'm just in port for one night, wanna dance?* She was fine-boned, but beneath her ribbed tank top he saw a hint of ropy muscle that suggested she did more than laundry in her spare time.

Her reddish-blond hair puffed into a curly mass around her head, and that, combined with her high cheekbones and wide mouth, made him think of the rarest of veil-tailed koi, a delicate fish once cherished by emperors and kept specially in shade-dappled pools where they were revered for their elegance and thought to bring good fortune in love.

Since Brody had learned long ago—rather painfully—that women don't like being compared to fish, he kept that observation to himself. Instead he offered her a hand up, which she declined, choosing to push herself up from the floor and dust herself off. And who could blame her? He'd almost knocked her down the stairs. She probably thought he'd help her up and accidentally toss her out a window.

"Sorry?" he offered hopefully. "I didn't mean to trample you, it was just that I—"

"Had more important things on your mind," she finished for him, which wasn't what he'd meant to say. "Don't worry, I'm used to it." And she turned and marched down the stairs with an iron rod down her back the size of *Streaker*'s longwave antenna. "Breakfast's in the dining room when you're ready, Mr. Davenport." And she was gone.

"Brr," Brody said to nobody in particular, unless one counted the fat orange cat that appeared out of the far bedroom to twine about his ankle. "That was pretty chilly. Wonder what I did?" Then he grinned. Miz Maddy sure was cute. Maybe the three weeks or so Dolphin Friendly was landbound for this project wouldn't be so bad after all.

He wasn't bored yet, and as his father had pointed out at depressingly regular intervals throughout his adolescence, Brody got bored easily, which is why he'd never amount to much of anything.

But as luck would have it, Dolphin Friendly had been a perfect fit from the moment the three friends had landed their first funding. Just as Brody, Smitty, and Violet were getting bored with each new place, each new port, it was time to move on to something else. Someone else.

Brody smoothed a hand across his freshly laundered pants and wondered whether Maddy—who struck him as the home and hearth type—would find it strange none of her new guests were married. But it was the nature of the job—he knew that even if an innkeeper might not.

Smitty's grad school marriage had failed because of his mobile lifestyle, and neither Brody nor Violet had ever come close to being hooked. Unencumbered, the three of them plus a few interns per year made up Dolphin Friendly, and their reputation had grown to such that they were up for a huge federal grant based partly on their work in Smuggler's Cove.

Brody grinned at the thought. That should impress her. Then he stopped. Why was he thinking of impressing her at all? He wasn't starting anything with her, even if she did remind him of a royal koi. Between Dolphin Friendly and the impending grant proposal, he was busier than a bottlenose in a bathtub full of mackerel. And besides, if he and his old man agreed on one thing, it was that Brody would make a terrible husband.

Husband? Who said anything about getting married? Brody missed a step and almost crushed the cat. But it stood to reason he'd be thinking that way, because Maddy Jamison had that look about her—the one that made him think of family, of freshly cooked meals and silver on the dining room table, of mortgages and mowing lawns. She had an air about her that reminded him of long-term things like marriage and kids, and made him picture *Streaker* sitting idle at the dock, or leaving without him for adventures untold with a new captain at her helm.

Then that same breeze wandered through the open window of his room and slid across his cheek with tickling fingers, and Brody grimaced when he heard the tinkle of Maddy's laughter from the kitchen below.

"Another lifetime, another man," he said to nobody in particular. "Too bad."

"You can't kick him out, he just got here." Levi's words were reasonable, but Maddy didn't want to hear it. They sat at her kitchen table drinking tea—Earl Grey for her, nuts and twigs for him—and discussing her guest.

"I just don't think it's going to work. He's been living on a boat for too long to act like a civilized human being. That's what happens." Maddy leaned toward Levi and gestured with her spoon to emphasize the point while her dratted hair swung forward and dipped itself in her tea as if it wanted a drink.

"You're on a boat day in and day out for so long with the same people that normal lines start to get blurred. The next thing you know, everyone's wearing wetsuits and knocking each other over." She nodded decisively. "When the rest of them get here, they'll probably act like that, too."

Levi choked on his tea and waved a graceful hand in front of his narrow face. "Can I come over? Sounds like my kind of party. Besides, Chrissy said that you said Davenport had a nice rear end."

Maddy was trying to come up with a fitting reply when there was a noise from the dining room and the door swung inward to reveal Brody Davenport standing at the threshold.

Though she'd seen him briefly not twenty minutes earlier, Maddy still thought he looked amazing—for a marine biologist, of course. He'd shaved, and there was a fresh nick on his chin right over the jagged mark on his jaw. Where had he gotten that scar?

Her mind instantly conjured up images of a dashing pirate rescuing the non–frizzy-haired damsel from a sneering villain, gaining an honorable wound in the process.

Nah, the rational part of her brain asserted, he probably got scarred in a bar fight like her brother Tiger had. She grimaced. Or caught a wayward bait hook with his face. Or was hit by a swinging boom. She, of anyone, knew the inherent dangers of life on the sea.

As she watched, Brody ran a hand through his still-damp hair and grinned, which made her heart go thumpety-thump. Then he turned and glanced at his own posterior, which made her thumping heart sink as she remembered just what she and Levi had been discussing.

Oh, no, just how much of that did he hear?

"Am I interrupting something?" Brody included Levi in his grinning question. "I don't mean to, but there was a rumor of food down here."

Maddy started to reply, though she had no idea how she was going to talk herself out of this one, but was interrupted when her throat seized up and she sneezed mightily. Twice.

The smell of flowers in the kitchen was overwhelming, choking her with its cheerfully cloying fragrance. She sneezed again and her eyes began to water. "What on earth is in that tea of yours, a nursery?" she asked Levi as she ran to open the door and shove back the curtains over the sink.

Levi sniffed his cup and shook his head. "It's not me, darling. Same old nuts and twigs in here as always."

"It's me."

Maddy turned to Brody, startled. "You wear perfume? Uh—I mean, a floral aftershave?" He didn't seem the type. If she had to pick a scent for him, it would be something spicy and manly with a hint of the hated ocean. Not flowers.

"Not exactly." He lifted his arm very deliberately and sniffed at the cuff of his shirt. He wrinkled his nose, deepening the lines at his eyes and drawing Maddy's attention to those thick, dark lashes again. "I think somebody got a little carried away with the fabric softener."

The laundry. Maddy gasped and inhaled another lungful of flowers, which sent her into a sneezing fit, which set her to laughing until tears came to her eyes in earnest. "I'm so sorry. It was the fish . . ."

She took a big gulp of tea to settle her quivering throat, and wound up scalding her tongue—which was probably no less than she deserved. "I hate the smell of fish, so I put extra detergent in the wash."

"Extra detergent?"

She nodded. "And some fabric softener." She sneezed. "And some deodorizer."

Levi snickered. "And some of that awful perfume you inherited along with the Inn when Grammie Jamison died a few years ago?"

"I'm sorry," she repeated helplessly in Brody's direction. "The clothes from your knapsack are done if you'd like to change later. I think I went easier with them. Why don't you sit down in the

'oom and I'll bring you coffee and some
t?"

.. gianced back the way he had come. "It's
big and lonely out there. Can I sit in here with
you two?" He grinned and her heart fluttered in
her chest like a minnow.

Unable to think of a plausible reason why he
shouldn't sit in the kitchen, Maddy sighed and
waved Brody to a seat at the kitchen table. She
poured coffee in a cup she chose at random from
the cabinet.

The kitchen seemed to shrink with him in it,
becoming intimate and cozy, and Maddy could
hardly move between the refrigerator and the
stove without brushing against him.

She wished he had picked the dining room instead of choosing to invade her kitchen. But she
would make him feel welcome as her grandmother would expect—with the dignity befitting
a Jamison.

Ever since her Nana had run the kitchen and
young Maddy and Marcus Jr. had helped their
Grampie with the fishing tours, the Smuggler's
Inn had served breakfast and dinner, and could
be persuaded to pack lunches as well.

Though the fishing tours were long gone, as
were both her grandparents, Maddy still served
two meals a day on her Nana's earthenware
dishes. The dining room was still presided over

by a portrait of her grandparents that had been painted in France after her Grampie Jamison was released from the Army and married his nurse, a pretty country girl who emigrated with him to his hometown on Cape Cod.

Another portrait had hung in the dining room at one time, but Maddy had removed the photo of herself, Marcus Jr., and their parents long ago and replaced it with the love that shone from the painting of a young soldier and his bride.

Although the guests that came as couples or families usually preferred to eat in the dining room, most of the single men and women wanted to eat in the kitchen with Maddy and whichever of her friends had stopped by for a bite.

She enjoyed getting to know the travelers that stayed with her, particularly her repeat customers, and had politely but firmly turned down advances from several bachelor guests and one married one as well.

Maddy had run the Inn for going on nine years now. She was used to handling her guests, even the whiny and demanding ones. So why did Brody's presence in her kitchen make her feel jumpy and frizzy and so very self-conscious?

Glancing quickly to make sure neither of the men was paying attention, Maddy tugged at her T-shirt, trying to straighten the collar and tuck it into the waistband of her jeans simultaneously. It wasn't until she pushed a chunk of her hair behind her left ear for the second time that she caught Levi's smirk out of the corner of her eye.

The rat. She glared at him and mouthed a dire threat over Brody's head if her friend so much as mentioned her fussing.

She handed Brody his coffee and ignored the jolt that ran the length of her arm when his fingers brushed hers.

Why did it irk her the way he settled right in at the table and introduced himself to Levi? Why did the kitchen seem smaller than it had before he walked in?

She scowled. Why didn't he just go back where he came from and leave her alone?

"Is this a hint?" Davenport raised the coffee cup in a mocking salute and she saw that she had given him the mug Chrissy's six-year-old daughter had given her for Christmas.

It had big, ugly flowers painted all over it, and it looked just like Davenport smelled. Levi guffawed, subsiding when Maddy glared.

Brody waved aside her spluttered apology, and Maddy turned back to the stove, happy to hide her hot face on the pretext of scrambling eggs. What was with her? She'd been around plenty of men, in her lifetime—well, a few anyway—and none of them had turned her into a blithering, stumbling, frizzy-haired idiot. She had to get a grip.

He's one of them, she told herself. *Remember that if nothing else.*

Brody chatted easily with Levi about the Yoga Palace, the place down on the boardwalk that Levi owned and ran, and Maddy smiled slightly at her guest's easy acceptance of her flamboyant friend.

"So you'll bring the Dolphin Friendlies over to my place for a class?" Levi asked. Maddy could just imagine what her friends would say about that.

"Sure," Brody agreed readily. "We do some basic positions on the boat a couple times a week when things are slow, usually led by my tech specialist, Violet. She'll be glad to learn a few more things to add to our routine, and the dolphins'll get a kick out of some new music."

"Dolphins?" Levi's voice rose in fascination. He loved watching the slippery creatures play in Smuggler's Cove and was forever trying to get Maddy to tag along, but she categorically refused to go near the water.

She lived near the sea because she couldn't bear to part with her grandparents' beloved Inn, and because Smuggler's Cove had more good memories for her than bad. But that didn't mean she had to swim in the ocean. Ever.

She spooned eggs onto three plates and arranged buttered bagels and pan-fried potatoes on two of them and whole wheat, organic toast on a third, knowing Levi's preferences well.

"Sure," Brody continued, still talking about doing yoga on board a boat. The very idea made Maddy nauseous and she transferred some of her eggs to Davenport's plate. "One of the groups we observed off St. John would gather when they heard our music and the juveniles spy-hopped to look in the boat. I think they found it funny. Step aerobics, especially if the music had a lively beat, set them to jumping and whistling."

She heard Brody shift in his chair and she imagined the light of enthusiasm in his eyes as he leaned forward in his eagerness to share the magic of the sea with another person.

Just like her father used to.

She almost bobbled the plate of eggs as Marcus Jamison's image came to her across the years, a face frozen forever on the portrait she kept wrapped up in the attic, as far away from her as she could get it.

"You see that, Princess?" He always called her Princess because his beloved wife and diving partner was The Queen. He pointed to a triangular fin that rose from the water with beautiful arrogance. "That's what we're here for. That's the big guy we're here to dance with."

Here was the Great Barrier Reef, and her father's new friend was an enormous great white shark. A maneater.

"Maddy?"

She had a feeling that Levi had been trying to get her attention for quite some time and she made a conscious effort to shake off the uncertain mood that memory had brought on. "I'm sorry. I was . . . never mind."

Levi looked at her in concern. "Are you okay? You're sort of pale and those eggs are getting colder by the minute."

"Oh. Sorry." She set Levi's plate in front of him and turned back for Davenport's breakfast. He was still talking animatedly about his work, and Maddy wondered if it would be rude to take her plate to her room.

When she went to set her guest's breakfast in front of him, he was in the process of rolling up his left sleeve. "And this is where a little one took a nibble out of me off the coast of St. John a few summers ago."

High up on his forearm, a semicircular scar stood out in sharp relief to the deep tan and dark hair of the rest of his arm. A shark bite.

Maddy sucked a breath and jerked back from the table at the sight of the scar.

The waters of her memory frothed white, then

pink, then stilled to clear as glass and Maddy saw her mother's face, beautiful and kind.

Time seemed to slow. Maddy saw the men look at her in concern as the floor tilted beneath her feet like the deck of a ship, saw Davenport's mouth move but heard no sound over the rushing in her ears, over the sound of waves.

The plate dropped from her suddenly nerveless fingers and bounced once on the kitchen table, seeming to hover there for the count of two or three before it flipped over and landed on Brody Davenport's lap.

He leapt up and she jerked back, stammering an apology that he quickly cut off. "Gosh, Maddy. I told you I was sorry for knocking you over, you didn't have to throw eggs on me!" But when he saw that his attempt at humor had failed, Brody's eyes turned more serious. "What's wrong?"

His eyes followed hers down to the scar and he raised his forearm. "Is it this? It wasn't much, just a little shark bite. I'm sorry if I startled you."

Seeming oblivious to the eggs dripping off his shirt and pants, Brody took a step toward her and she leaped back. "This isn't going to work," she began. "I can't do this. I want you—"

Out of here, she'd meant to say, but was interrupted by a brisk ring of the phone. She grabbed the handset and answered automatically, listened a moment, and handed the phone to her unwanted guest while her stomach sank to her toes. "For you. It's Mr. Smith."

Eyes never leaving hers, Davenport took the phone. "Smitty? This isn't such a good time . . . What? You're kidding, that's great! But wait, hold on a minute."

He covered the mouthpiece and spoke to Maddy. "My group finished their prep work early and got on the road ahead of schedule—which is a first for us, by the way—and, well, what were you going to say just now?"

Levi poked her in the ribs, and Maddy grimaced when the ghost of Grannie Jamison whispered, *"They have reservations,"* as though that solved everything. But in a way, it did. Like it or not, Dolphin Friendly was depending on her to be an innkeeper and Maddy couldn't let them— or her grandmother—down, regardless of her own personal feelings. She heaved a big sigh and pasted a false-feeling smile on her face.

"Nothing, Mr. Davenport. I was going to suggest that you head upstairs and change into some egg-free clothes."

Yeah, right, said his eyes, but out loud he merely asked, "Are you sure?" and when she nodded he spoke quickly into the phone, confirming their reservations and checking on the status of his equipment and his boat.

The words flowed over Maddy, familiar terms she had once used as easily as breathing. She closed her eyes against the swift jab of pain, opening them only to ask, "When will they be here?"

But when she heard the cheerful tootle of an unfamiliar horn and the blatting of a diesel engine fouling her flowerbeds as a big, dented pickup crunched its way up the clamshell drive, Maddy didn't need Davenport to tell her.

"They're here."

Chapter Three

Followed by Levi, Maddy made her way outside on rubbery legs and found her worst fears confirmed. There was a circus in her driveway. A salty, watery circus the likes of which Smuggler's Cove hadn't seen in nine years.

Next to Brody's Jeep sat a crew cab truck, its bed piled high with boxes and bags and stacks of folded things. A Zodiac crouched atop the heap, secured by an impressive array of bungee cords and rope. Behind the truck there was a small trailer carrying a stubby, awkward contraption with bulging glass windows sprouting in all directions.

Six strangers stood ranged in front of the vehicle, far too many to have all fit in the truck, and Maddy glanced past Mary Jo's to the Smuggler's Cove Marina and saw that sure enough, there was a new vessel berthed at Big Jim's Pier next to his nephew's fishing skiff. The strange boat's superstructure bristled with antennae and an additional Zodiac lurked on its deck. Looking from humans to boat and back again, Maddy came to the reluctant conclusion that like it or not, she couldn't possibly back out now.

Dolphin Friendly had arrived, and they were staying.

What had she really meant to say? Brody watched Maddy welcome her new guests with the same polished manners she'd used when he showed up a day early, covered with fish guts, and wondered what had happened between them in the kitchen. She'd been afraid of something, but what? He glanced briefly at the mark on his arm, a permanent reminder of the diver's litany *check and double-check.* It had been a small shark, and in all honesty his own fault, but he supposed the scar might startle a groundhog like his landlady. It was funny, though. Maddy Jamison hadn't struck him as the type to be scared by a little imperfection here and there.

At least he hoped she wasn't, or she'd be pretty horrified once she met the rest of Dolphin Friendly.

"Bored yet?" A rude elbow shoved itself into Brody's ribs and he didn't need to look to identify its owner.

"Smitty." The word was neither a greeting nor an answer. In fact, Brody was seriously considering sending the whole crew back up north for a few days on some trumped-up excuse so he could have more time alone with Maddy—time to explore the fleeting moment of attraction between them in the upstairs hall that morning. He was sure he hadn't imagined it. He couldn't have.

But he also couldn't send the team away. The Smuggler's Cove Project was too important in the long term to sacrifice for a woman he barely knew.

Long term. Brody paused. When had he begun to think about the future? Usually he was the first one off and running to the next venue, the next port, the next project. He was the doer, not the planner. Brody Davenport. A human tornado. A whirling dervish who touched down in this place or that, never staying long, never tying himself down.

Never thinking about what came next.

When had that stopped being enough? Brody wondered as he stared at the front of the Inn. When had life on the road become boring? He wasn't sure, just that it had. He was tired of always being on the move, living out of a suitcase or a boat.

Yikes.

Smitty's eyes followed Maddy up the porch steps as she led the new interns, Ahab and Ishmael, up to their bunks. "Yep. I can see that things around here are going to be downright dull for the next three weeks."

Out of the corner of his eye, Brody saw Maddy's shoulders stiffen and knew she'd missed the sarcasm in Smitty's comment. She hurried into the house before Brody said, "Shut up, Smitty. And hands off. She's a nice lady."

"Didn't say she wasn't." Smitty dug his hands in his pants pockets and rocked back on his heels. "Just taking your temperature. Since it seems lukewarm at best, I think I'll go on in and introduce myself to our pretty Miss Jamison. I'm sure you won't object."

Smitty pretended to duck and seemed disappointed when Brody didn't swing. He shrugged, whistled an obnoxious little ditty, and trotted up the front steps of the house shouting, "Yoo-hoo! Honey, I'm home!"

Brody turned away from the Inn and looked at *Streaker* where she rested grandly at Big Jim's Pier. *The Smuggler's Cove Project,* he reminded himself. *That's why you're here.* He wasn't in Smuggler's Cove for a brief romance—the only kind he allowed himself. He was in Smuggler's Cove to secure his future and that of the thousands of marine mammals that depended on groups like Dolphin Friendly for conservation. He had a job to do, and it didn't include romancing the innkeeper.

Whistling a wistful tune of his own, Brody followed his team into the Smuggler's Inn. He already missed the quiet.

As she helped her new guests settle into their rooms, Maddy had the distinct impression that things were rapidly spinning out of her control and she wasn't sure how to regain her footing. She'd lost her kerchief in the first flurry of activity and her flyaway hair made her feel completely scattered. Even worse, an unnatural awareness of Brody Davenport hovered at the edge of her consciousness and made her skin prickle.

Forcing Davenport from her immediate thoughts, she put Mr. Smith, a tall redhead with a happy twinkle in his eye and a ready smile on his lips, in the master suite as he had requested. Although it was clear that as the group leader Brody ought to have the room with the private bath, Maddy figured she'd let Mr. Smith—"Call me Smitty, please"—work that out with his boss.

The pair of fresh-faced grad students bunked together. They introduced themselves as Ahab and Ishmael, though the darker of the two admitted that his name was really Peter and that he had been nicknamed Ahab when he became friends with Ishmael. They reminded Maddy of her brother when he'd been a postdoc and she a second-year grad student.

The last summer they'd worked together. The summer their parents died.

She shook the memory off and went on with the room assignments. Luckily—because she was having mild palpitations at the thought of having seven members of Dolphin Friendly stay at the Inn when the reservation only called for five— the two crew members responsible for the boat planned to sleep there. The man and woman, whose names Maddy didn't catch, assured her they were happier sleeping at sea.

That left Violet. Maddy could tell right away the woman was going to be trouble. After almost ten years of running the Inn, first assisting her grandparents, then alone after their retirement, Maddy had a pretty good sense of which customers were going to need extra coddling, which were going to complain no matter what she did, and which were just plain nasty.

She wasn't sure which of the categories would hold the sleek, perfectly made-up Violet, but she knew for certain that the woman was going to be difficult. Within the first five minutes, Violet had made snippy comments about the shared bathroom, the bed, the curtains, the town, and Maddy's hair. "So unfortunate what the sea air does to naturally curly hair, isn't it, dear?"

Thankfully, Smitty came to Maddy's rescue before she disgraced her grandmother's memory and slugged a guest. The lanky redhead deftly insulted Violet out of her sulk and bullied her into walking down to the beach. Smitty sent Maddy a telling eye-roll on the way out the door, making her grin.

"That one's going to be a real treat to have around," Maddy muttered to herself, envisioning three more weeks of catty bad-hair comments from the brunette.

"Talking to yourself, Princess?" Brody's already familiar voice from behind her was startling, but no more so than the endearment.

She spun around and looked up at his silty blue-green eyes. "What did you call me? Why did you call me that?"

He shrugged lazily and flicked a finger over an enthusiastic curl. "Princess just seems appropriate, that's all. You object?"

Did she object? How could she, when he said the word with a silky slide, as if it really meant something to him that he have a nickname for her that nobody else did.

Nobody except a man long dead. A man she had once loved.

Her father.

"No, I—"

"Brody?" Ishmael stuck his head into the hallway and the mood—if that's what it had been—between them was broken. Mussed and confused, Maddy beat a quick retreat while Brody answered his intern's question about the SSM they would use for mapping the cove. Though she knew well what the Semi-Submersible Seasickness Machine was and what it did, she considered the knowledge more curse than a gift, and as she took refuge in her private suite, Maddy feared that the next three weeks would be the same.

His voice had floated down the stairs after her. "I'll catch you later, Princess."

Princess.

"Be good, Princess," her mother had caroled long ago. "We're off to the islands because the turtles and the sharks miss us."

"But Mommy, *I'll* miss you. You just got home." Ten-year-old Maddy had known she was whining, but she didn't care. Thirteen-year-old Tiger had stood at his sister's side, glowering at their parents.

Pammy Jamison had knelt by her daughter while Marcus Sr. loaded the van. "I know, Princess. But we have work to do. You know your father gets bored staying home—he needs the sea to be happy."

"I'll make him happy, Mommy. I'll be very good if you stay home, at least until the science fair." Maddy felt her brother take her hand in support and knew there was no hope.

"Madelyne, that's enough. Kiss your mother and give me a hug like a good girl. We'll send you something nice from Hawaii if you behave for your grandparents." Marcus Sr. shook his son's hand and hugged his daughter tight. "We'll come back, Princess. I promise."

And they had. That time.

Dinner was noisy, as it almost always was when Dolphin Friendly ate as a unit, made more so by the excitement of finally starting the all-important project. The crew crowded around a big table in the dining room and shouted over one another as necessary to make relevant and irrelevant points.

Seated at the head of the table—having booted his assistant from the position—Brody watched Maddy out of the corner of his eye as he ate. She flitted around unobtrusively, making sure that the large bowls of salad and bread were always full and that there was meatloaf and pasta for all. Although there was a place set for her, she was seldom seated for more than a minute before she was up again, seeing to her guests' pleasure with calm efficiency.

The conversation around the table was lively, and as it always did amongst marine researchers, eventually swam to the topic of fish.

"My Grannie on the bayou side of the family made an incredible blackened catfish," Smitty reminisced while loading his plate for the third time. He could eat all day long and never gain an ounce, much to Violet's loud annoyance. "All peppery and spicy and ready to melt in your mouth."

Everyone except Maddy made appreciative noises.

"Maybe sometime in the next few weeks we could drop a line while we're out in the Cove and catch dinner." Brody could see Smitty warming to his idea even as Maddy shrank in her seat and turned a delicate shade of lavender.

"Are you okay?" he asked quietly, beneath the chatter of the others.

"Yeah," Smitty continued, "I'm pretty sure it's Violet's turn to gut dinner, and I'll see if I can reproduce Grannie's spicy batter, and—"

Maddy gulped audibly and Brody shushed the other man. "Princess, what's wrong?"

"I-I don't much care for the smell of fish."

Brody nodded, remembering her comment that morning over breakfast that she'd perfumed his clothes to get rid of the smell of fish. "Right. Sorry, I forgot." He turned to Smitty and tried to redirect the conversation before things got sticky. "No fish in the house. New subject?"

"What's wrong with fish?" This from Ahab, who should have been smart enough to keep his trap shut.

"I don't like fish." Maddy's voice got stronger. "In fact, I hate fish—the smell of them, the taste of them, everything." She shuddered as though she could feel them sliding across her skin. "You're welcome to cook as many fish as you want outside on the grill, but I'd prefer not to have them in my home."

Violet got that look in her eye, the one she got right before she nailed Smitty with one of her so-called practical jokes, and Brody cringed. Her voice insinuated itself into the conversation, sweet as honey, pointed as a knife. "But, Maddy, dear, isn't it hard to spend time down on the beach if you don't like the smell of fish?"

Maddy shook her head. "I don't go down to the beach. I don't like the ocean."

There was silence then as the members of Dolphin Friendly tried to process that statement, tried to dissect it like a specimen under the stereoscope, and Brody felt Violet's eyes latch on to him before they slid over to Smitty. She smiled nastily.

"Oh dear, Brody." Her voice was, if possible, even sweeter than it had been. "She doesn't like the water. Isn't that a shame?"

Not long after dinner, Brody cornered his assistant in an upstairs bedroom. "What's wrong with Violet?"

Smitty rolled his eyes, then rolled his head on his neck a few times to relieve the kink Brody knew came from driving the pickup long distances. "Today, or in general?" The redhead dropped onto his bed and stretched out amidst the mass of fluffy pillows that was piled high on each guest bed. "Where should I start?"

The three had been fast friends since grad school, and Brody and Violet had dated half-heartedly for a time, but she and Smitty had a strange sort of adversarial friendship that seemed to work well for them, and Brody wasn't above using it. "Can you ask her to lay off Maddy? She's not one of us, and she shouldn't have to suffer Violet's version of constructive criticism, you know?"

Smitty grinned suddenly, affectionately. "When we were out on a shakedown cruise with *Streaker* the other night, Violet hit the rough weather horn in the wee hours of the morning. You should've seen it—the interns came stumbling up half-asleep and she told them the best way to get to the lifeboats on the port side was to jump over the railing and catch the ladder on the way down."

Brody snickered. "There isn't a ladder on the port side."

"No lifeboats, either," Smitty agreed. "Don't worry, we fished them out pretty quickly. No harm done."

"Not to them, that's part of being in Dolphin Friendly, but Maddy . . ."

Smitty nodded. "You're right. I'll talk to Violet, but you owe me." They were both well acquainted with their teammate's dislike of being told what to do.

"You got the room with the toilet, didn't you? I think that makes us even," Brody reminded him.

"Yeah. You've got a point there," Smitty allowed. "But, boss, in her own special way Violet brought up a good point. What's with the landlady and fish?"

Brody shrugged. "Dunno. She doesn't like them, I guess. Who can explain landers? Anyway, why don't you go talk to Violet?

Smitty grumbled and left, but Brody stayed in the room and leaned partway out the open window. Why did Maddy hate the smell of fish? It was inconceivable to him that anyone could hate the smell of fish. It was a complex odor, and to the trained nose could speak volumes about an ecosystem's delicate balance or a marine mammal's diet. Sure it could be pungent. But repulsive? That was hard to believe.

Besides, she lived near Smuggler's Cove, one of the most interesting marine habitats in the Northeast. Who could fail to appreciate the wonder of that?

On the rocky islands in the Cove, gaggles of plump spotted harbor seals bore their pups. Farther out to sea swam the wise old humpbacks, the long, sleek fin whales, and their Minke brethren.

And closer to the shore, where the SSM and *Streaker* would spend much of their time, lived the special friends of Dolphin Friendly—a noisy, raucous group of dolphins and porpoises that were Brody's personal favorites.

All of it outside the window, down past Smuggler's Point, under the surface of the cold North Atlantic waters where he and his wetsuited crew would go. Brody placed his hands on the windowsill, looked down to the twilit beach, and yearned for the work to begin. He strained toward the heaving water, imagined the cool slide against his skin, prepared himself for that thrill of contact when a curious dolphin would check to see what sort of creature had come into its wet world spewing bubbles from its face and bumbling about on two fins when a single fluke worked so much better.

Then a trill of sound distracted him from his cool, blue fantasy and brought him back to the ruddy glow of twilight at the Smuggler's Inn. Looking down, he saw Maddy weeding the flowerbeds next to her back door and he wondered whether she was working outside because she needed to use every ounce of daylight to get her work done, or because she was trying to escape from the full Inn. She sang as she worked, something sweet and happy about earth and land, and he watched her for the pleasure of it as the cool ghost of the ocean faded from his senses.

She paused every now and then, to wipe her brow with a red bandana, to chat with a friend passing by on the boardwalk, or to smile at the fat orange cat that twined itself around her ankles. But as he watched with unashamed curiosity, Brody noticed one thing that made him think back to her dislike of the smell of fish and her reaction to the scar on his arm.

Though the blood-red sun gleamed off the sawgrass that marched its way over the nearby dunes, a group of children squealed as they played flashlight tag down by the water, and a flock of herring gulls flapped and swore at each other as they fought for the choicest bits amongst seaweed left by the tide, Maddy seemed oblivious to the show being put on just behind her.

She gardened and chatted with her friends, but

it was as if they ceased to exist once they passed over the hump of the dunes that separated the town from the sea. She never once looked down to the sparsely populated beach, nor did she watch the stately old ketch sail into the cove and tie up at Big Jim's Pier next to *Streaker*.

"I'll be dipped in oil and pan fried like calamari," he said, and whistled down low. "She's afraid of the ocean." She'd all but told him as much, but something in Brody had fought the idea. Denied it, because he didn't want it to be true. Because he could never be with a woman who didn't love the sea.

Brody looked toward his ocean. The waves thundered against the jetty at Smuggler's Point and hissed along the shore as Maddy finished her weeding and bent down to gather her tools. Denim stretched across her hips and her reddish hair escaped the scarf and fell forward, shading her face so that Brody felt safe watching her.

Felt safe wishing it could be otherwise.

Chapter Four

"So now they're all convinced that I'm nuts. *He's* especially convinced, because how could any normal, red-blooded, reasonably attractive woman in his universe not like the ocean?" Maddy snapped the sheet across Violet's bed with unnecessary vigor and Marmalade wrinkled his whiskered nose.

"I know, I know. I should've kept my mouth shut. But how could I? There's no way I'm letting them cook fish in my kitchen."

The fat orange creature batted a lazy paw while Maddy fluffed the pillows and settled the duvet, then stretched slinkily in that boneless way tabbies have, as if to say, *So what's the big deal? I like fish.*

"Of course you do, you're a cat. I'm not a cat and I don't like fish—not one bit—and maybe it's best Brody found that out sooner than later." And Maddy heard her own words and sat down hard on the freshly made bed.

"Well, that was egotistical of me, wasn't it? He hasn't made move one and I'm already warning him off. I should be ashamed of myself." But she wasn't. It felt good to find a man besides Kevin even briefly interesting. Maybe there was hope for her after all.

Then she remembered why she wasn't interested, remembered who Brody Davenport actually was, and she gave Violet's throw pillow an unnecessarily vicious punch. "Never mind. His crew's here now and I'll be lucky to see a minute of him between now and the day they leave—not that I want to see him, of course."

She tossed the pillow on the bed, and Marmalade scooted out of the way just in time, fluffing his tail indignantly. "Well, at least they're not too messy with their clothes and their equipment," Maddy commented as she and the cat went to make up Smitty's room.

She thought she'd save Brody's for last.

"I sure hope you know what you're doing." Smitty's voice echoed hollowly from within the Semi-Submersible Seasickness Machine and

Brody pulled himself out from underneath the trailer to answer.

"Of course I know what I'm doing. I built this thing from scratch, remember?" The SSM had been part of his thesis and he'd kept it with him over the years, not having found a better way to scan large areas of water than to lie facedown in the odd little vehicle and look out the bulbous windows as it was towed behind *Streaker.*

"I'm not talking about the SSM, boss. It's fine, just needed a new seal around the lower viewport and a couple of bolts on the starboard stabilizer. We're good as gold to start the cove this morning." Smitty tugged a pair of air tanks from underneath the Zodiac in the back of the pickup truck and tossed them on the trailer with the SSM.

"Then what're you talking about? I know what I'm doing—starting probably the biggest project we've ever tackled. Think of it, Smitty—a computer model that'll integrate the phases of the moon, the temperature of the water, the prevalent winds, the position of food fish, and the topography of the area and maybe, just maybe give us an idea where we'll be needed next." Brody could feel the excitement tingle in his fingertips, heard the sea calling, *It's time to go!*

"I am thinking about it, boss."

"Then what're you babbling about?"

Smitty waited until Brody looked his way, then jerked his chin at the Inn, where lace curtains fluttered and the men could just hear a sweet trill of melody from one of the upstairs rooms. "Her. I saw the way you were looking at her this morning at breakfast."

"Maddy? I wasn't—well, maybe I was looking, but why not? She's a beautiful woman." She was a heck of a lot more than that, but he wasn't sure he had the words yet to describe how the innkeeper continued to draw him in spite of their differences.

Smitty paused before answering. "She's not your usual type, boss."

"You said you liked her." Irritated by the conversation, Brody wrestled with the bungee cords that secured the Zodiac to the truck. He almost caught a hook in the eye for his troubles, stopped, and took a calming breath. "So what's the problem?"

"She's not one of us, Brody. She'll never be one of us and you know it. You'll break her heart."

It wasn't so much the words that stilled his hand. It was Smitty's use of his given name—an occasion that was tantamount to his mother's use of his middle name. It meant serious business.

"I wasn't planning to—" Brody stopped himself because he had been planning on asking

Maddy to walk with him that evening when the sun went down—if the team had made landfall, of course. "I wouldn't hurt her," he finished lamely.

"You wouldn't mean to," Smitty corrected. "But you probably would anyway. What do you think? That she's the kind of woman who'll welcome one night of romance, or even three weeks of it? Or longer? What if we stay the summer and model all the way out to Stellwagen Bank? Think she'll be glad to wave good-bye when fall comes? I think not."

Brody looked across the yard, stared at the pretty flowers and the growing lawn. "But what if—"

"There is no 'what if', boss. When guys like us get involved with women like that it can only lead to trouble. Trust me, I know."

Smitty had once been married to an agronomy student—the proverbial farmer's daughter—and left her behind when they went to sea. One stormy February night when they returned to port, Ellen had met her husband on the dock to tell him that she was divorcing him and moving in with an organic pig farmer.

Since then he'd been more than leery of relationships between marine field biologists and landers. In fact, Brody thought, Smitty hadn't been much of a relationship advocate in general, so he countered, "Yeah, but if I did it your way, I'd be a monk. What's your motto these days? 'I don't date non-marine biologists, and I don't date marine biologists'? There's not much left to work with."

The tips of Smitty's ears pinkened slightly but he was saved from replying when a single, ear-splitting scream sounded from behind one of the fluttering lace curtains.

Maddy! Every neuron that Brody possessed, including a few he hadn't known about before, fired to life simultaneously and he was across the driveway and up the porch before Smitty had even turned toward the house.

Imagining burglary, murder, black-masked thugs with submachine guns and a couple of rabid German shepherds, Brody thundered up the carpeted stairs to the second floor and cast about frantically for Maddy. Where was she? Had they taken her? Was she even now drugged, slung over her attacker's shoulder, and on her way to be sold into slavery?

Then a streak of orange fur shot through a door and he took the cat's hint and bolted into Smitty's room.

Relief shuddered through him when he found Maddy pressed into the corner between the armoire and the wall, staring with fixed intensity at the floor next to the bed.

Without stopping to think, he pulled her into his arms, shielding her from whatever was on the bedroom floor. She burrowed into him like a small, curvy creature seeking warmth, and hid her face against his chest for one heartbeat. And another.

As his pulse returned to normal, Brody took a second look around the room and didn't see any black-robed ninjas crouched near Smitty's bed, nor did he see a chainsaw-wielding, hockey mask–wearing weirdo standing behind the open door.

In fact, he didn't see a darned thing out of place.

Slower than his boss, Smitty pounded into the room and slid to a halt, looking wild-eyed and brandishing a spear gun he'd taken from the lockbox in the Zodiac. "What? Where? Who—?"

Brody ducked under the wickedly barbed spear and disarmed Smitty before he harpooned one of the grinning teddy bears on the bureau. "Give that here! What're you trying to do, kill somebody?"

"It sounded like somebody was already dead! What the heck happened?" Smitty stared around the room in search of the rabid pack of wolves that had attacked their landlady. He too came up blank. "What happened?" he said, now sounding more confused than panicked.

"I—" Brody stopped. He had no idea. He

turned to ask Maddy and noticed that while he held the spear gun in one hand, his other arm was still wrapped around her, cradling her against his chest. He let her go and as she put some distance between them, he noticed that she no longer looked terrified.

She looked horribly, horribly embarrassed.

Maddy couldn't believe she'd screamed. She also couldn't believe that Brody had charged to her rescue like the proverbial white knight, or guardian angel, or prince or whatever. But she remembered quite clearly how nice it felt to have him hold her. How nice it had been to feel his heart beat fast under her cheek and realize he'd been worried.

He looked at her with those pretty eyes and grinned, finally relaxing. "What's the matter, Princess? You see a spider or something?"

She glared at him, knights and princes forgotten. "Don't patronize me, Davenport. I'm not afraid of spiders."

"Then what?"

Smitty followed Maddy's gaze to the floor beneath the bedside table, starting to get angry as she said, "There's a big, ugly dead fish under the bed. Is this some sort of a sick joke? Did your Violet think it would be funny to freak me out?"

"Oh no, Dusty!" Smitty bent down and scraped

what appeared to be a blob of mud off the floor and held it cupped gently in two palms.

Brody winced. "What the heck's Dusty doing in here? Where's his tank?"

Blushing, looking like a small boy caught with a pile of dirty magazines under his mattress, Smitty reached over to the bedside table, pushed two oceanography texts aside, and lifted a towel to reveal a small fish tank. "Back here. I didn't think Maddy'd find it here, so I was hoping . . ." He trailed off and looked up to see how mad she was.

His expression was so darned forlorn, and Maddy was sympathetic toward the loss of any pet—even a fish—so she instantly forgave him the hidden tank. "I guess it's okay. No harm done, I was more surprised than anything."

Smitty brightened. "Then I can keep him in here?"

What harm could it do to assure the distraught man that she would have allowed his pet if only it hadn't died? The thing was dry, motionless, and so covered with lint that she had almost swept it up as a dust bunny before she saw the fins and screamed, embarrassing herself and startling the men. So she shrugged. "I guess."

"Cool! Thanks!" Smitty blew on the inert creature and picked a few pieces of cat hair off it, then reached behind the hidden tank for a spray bottle of butter substitute.

"It's not Better Butter. He recycles the containers and fills them with Slime Kote." Brody's voice sounded low in her ear and she jumped, having not realized he was so close. She could feel his warm breath fluttering the hair behind her ear and a thrill of awareness shivered through her body while she watched Smitty lovingly spray the dead fish with Better Butter—er, Slime Kote.

"Slime Kote," she repeated dully, beginning to see where this was going.

"Great stuff," Smitty enthused. "It renews Dusty's natural skin and scale protection, which dries up after a few minutes out of the water. He can stay alive twenty minutes or so. Isn't that cool?"

He dropped the fish into the water. It sank to the bottom and lay like a slug.

"He'll be right as rain and swimming around in a jiff," Smitty predicted cheerfully. "Every now and again, particularly when we move to a new place, he'll sucker on to the side of the tank and just work his way up and out. Plecotamus like him'll do that from time to time. He's just lucky you found him! Much more than a half hour, and all the Slime Kote in the world wouldn't have helped."

"Great. Lucky." Maddy couldn't take her eyes

off the ugly brown sucker fish as it stirred sluggishly and flicked its tail a few times. Frankenfish returned from the dead.

"I thought we agreed you'd use the screen lid I got you," Brody observed mildly from behind Maddy's shoulder. The warmth of his body at her back waged war with the inner chill that always accompanied close encounters of the fishy kind.

"He didn't like the shade."

Dusty rose from the gravel at the bottom of his tank, bumbled into a green plant, and made a lurching circuit of the perimeter before latching on to the glass facing the three humans. The fleshy circle of his mouth sucked grotesquely and Maddy shivered. "He can't live on the boat?" Or in the toilet?

Smitty colored slightly. "Uh. Not really. He goes off his food and turns a funny shade of tan when he's on the boat. I'd rather not keep him there."

Brody coughed and she read amusement radiating along with his welcome body heat. She said, "Your fish gets seasick?" This couldn't be happening.

"You could say that." Smitty ducked his head and grinned. "Which is why I'm so grateful you said he could stay! Thank you, Maddy. You're a classy lady." Apparently deciding to retreat while he still held the upper hand, Brody's assistant kissed her cheek and ducked out the door with a quick, "I'll see you out at *Streak*, boss."

When he was gone, Maddy turned her back on the fish to confront Brody and was startled to see that he still held the spear gun.

Instantly, the image of him holding the weapon on the deck of his research vessel came to her. She pictured him wearing that shortie wetsuit she'd seen the other night. His arms and legs were bare and the flippers on his feet should have looked ridiculous but instead made him seem otherworldly, as if he was a creature of both land and water, equally comfortable with both.

In her imagination, the wetsuited hunk sketched her a cheery wave and tumbled backward into the cool blue water.

And was gone.

She shuddered and Brody placed the spear gun carefully on Smitty's bed before stepping closer to her. "Are you okay? About Dusty, I mean. He's really important to Smitty, so if the tank can stay here, I'd appreciate it. You can skip cleaning this room if that would help." He skimmed his hands up and down her arms and she shivered again at the sensation.

Something warm and furry twined around her ankles and she bent to pick up Marmalade, forcing Brody to drop his hands and step back. She held the cat in front of her like a shield and buried her nose in the orange fluff. Warm. Dry. Furry. Cats hated the water, hated the sea.

Cats also had nine lives. People didn't. People died.

"There isn't an ice cube's chance in the Gulf Stream of anything happening between us, is there?" Brody's voice echoed strangely in the room, as if the sea breeze, the calling gulls, the purring cat, and the bubbling fish tank had all stilled to listen.

Maddy just shook her head, though she wasn't sure whether she was agreeing or disagreeing. When Brody stepped back, he created a distance between them that was only a foot or so but felt like miles.

He retrieved the spear gun with one hand and held the other out to her in silent invitation. "Come with me out on the boat?"

"I can't. I'm sorry."

She shook her head slowly, denying more than just a morning out on the cove. She paused, then asked helplessly, "Stay with me here?" but she already knew what the answer would be.

"I can't. I'm sorry." Brody smiled sadly and touched her cheek before he left the room.

His footsteps crunched on the clamshell drive and she heard the hails and excited shouts from Big Jim's Pier a moment later as he rejoined his comrades. His people. His life.

Mechanically, Maddy tidied Smitty's room and found comfort in the familiar routine. When she reached the bedside table she found a screen behind it that fit on Dusty's tank. She piled the oceanography texts on top of the lid, just in case the creature sucked its way to freedom again and found the strength to push the lid aside.

She was patting the last pillow into place when she heard cheers as the big diesel engines spluttered to life. Although she told herself that she wouldn't, Maddy walked to the window and brushed the lace curtain aside.

For the first time in almost ten years, she watched a boat depart from Big Jim's Pier and churn its way out into the bright blue of Smuggler's Cove.

"May your winds run true and your skies stay fair," she murmured as she had when she was a child, watching her parents leave yet again. "And may the seas stay calm and your boat stay safe until I see you again."

She watched as *Streaker* rounded the last jetty and headed for open water, and she whispered an addition to her child's prayer. "And may the sharks swim away when you dive."

Chapter Five

And thus excited, an electron may jump from s-orbital to p-orbital such that—

"Argh!" Maddy slapped the text shut and wondered whether it would fit down the garbage disposal. Probably not.

She hated p-chem. It was stupid. *She* was stupid. What kind of a dumb idea was it anyway to go back to grad school at her age? And why bother with p-chem? She wasn't finishing her old degree—absolutely not. She should drop out of the stupid class and try something else.

Like basket weaving.

She banged her head against the kitchen table once for good measure, then stopped and sighed, pressing her forehead against the cool wood. P-chem wasn't the problem.

The problem was Dolphin Friendly. And Brody Davenport.

She looked across the table to the little carving he'd brought her the other day. "I saw this in a little store down the way," he'd said, casually dropping it on the table near her, "and it reminded me of you." She resisted the urge to reach out and stroke it. She remembered when Chrissy's husband Michael had carved the little statuette, how he had asked her to sit for him for an hour or so because he'd needed her face. When it was finished a week later, he'd showed it to her.

"I understand why you might not be thrilled. Christine told me about your parents, so I won't be offended if you don't want it."

Maddy had been shaken, but unable to deny the beauty of the piece. "It's lovely, Michael. But I thought you were going to carve Marmalade and me in the garden?"

Michael had shrugged. "That's what I thought I was going to carve, too. But the wood had other ideas." He spread his hands. "I don't argue with wood."

And so, regretfully, Maddy had passed up the little carving, only thinking of it now and then with a small pang of sadness. Last she'd heard

Link Shale had taken it for his "local artists" display at the Western wear store.

Now it was hers.

She gave in to temptation and ran her finger across the shape of a girl with a woman's curves and a cascade of curling hair that flowed down her shoulders and back to merge with the churning surf. From within that carved wave sprang the sinuous form of a playing dolphin and the woman's arms and legs tangled with the dolphin's flukes and fins until it seemed that there was no end to one or beginning of the other, but that there was just one entity, a woman-dolphin, frolicking in the ocean.

Brody's door upstairs opened then shut, jerking Maddy from her thoughts, and she yanked her hand away from the carving as if she had been caught doing something naughty. She heard his footsteps on the carpeted hallway above and when she heard the bathroom door close, wondered what he was doing. Was he headed to the shower in a wetsuit again?

She almost banged her head against the table another time, but instead ordered, "Get a grip, Madelyne. There's no way you're getting involved with Brody Davenport, so don't even think about it. In fact, you should be thinking about the p-chem exam next week. So get on with it."

Then the shower upstairs began to run and her concentration was completely shot. "Gah!" She lunged to her feet and grabbed a pile of books as though it was a lifeline. "I can't work like this. I can't study with that man in my house. I'm out of here."

But she slipped the carving into her pocket as she stomped out.

As she often did when she didn't know where else to go, Maddy went to Mary Jo's diner. She sat at a rear booth with her back to the room and her head buried in the textbook, just in case somebody thought about being friendly and joining her.

How was she going to survive the next few weeks with Brody and his crew in her home? The money she was making would help pay for school all right, but the point was moot if she failed p-chem so miserably that no respectable program would have her.

Her lunch arrived then, borne by none other than the head chef, Kevin Forster. Her ex-fiancé. "Hey, Mads. Why are you sulking back here?"

She pulled the textbook toward her nose. "I'm studying, not sulking. Go away, Kevin." She read fiercely for about thirty seconds before she dropped the book with a disgusted sigh. "Never mind. I'm sorry for snapping at you, I'm just useless today. I'm stupid, frustrated, and totally deranged."

Kevin shrugged and flicked a shaggy lock of hair away from his left eye, where she knew it would return momentarily. "No problem, Mads. What're friends for?"

"Well . . ." She tried to decide how much she should tell him. Did an ex-fiancé really want to know that she was completely consumed by thoughts of another man? Probably not.

He tapped the book on the top of the stack. "Is there something you need help with?"

She started to refuse, knowing that chemistry wasn't really his strong suit—in more ways than one—then realized Kev wasn't pointing to a chemistry text. He was indicating a cheerful red hardcover with sickeningly sweet cartoons capering around inch-high letters that proudly advertised *1,000 Best Baby Names.*

"Yikes!" She jumped and knocked the book off the pile. It landed smack-dab on top of the juicy Smuggler's Cove Burger she knew Kevin had prepared just the way she liked it.

Well, she thought philosophically, at least he hadn't brought her soup.

Kevin retrieved the book and wiped it off before returning it to her hands. "You were saying?"

She shook her head and chuckled. "Nothing. I

must've grabbed that book by mistake on my way out the door, and no, that was not a Freudian slip. This book is for Chrissy because she and Michael are battling over baby names. In her opinion, DeWalt is a fine name for a rotary sander, but not a child."

"Well, Mike is a woodcarver, after all. I suppose DeWalt is better than Craftsman when you come right down to it."

"Or Black and Decker," agreed Maddy, and they grinned at each other in the easy accord that made them good friends and eternally dull lovers.

Then Kevin sobered and leaned across her slightly flattened burger to cover her hands with his. "Seriously, Mads. Are you okay with these marine biologists staying with you?"

She squeezed Kev's hands, knowing that he truly cared. "I am. At least I'm okay with the money they're spending at the Inn." Not quite ready to talk to Kev about graduate school, she took a bite of her burger to buy herself a moment of chewing time. It was done perfectly of course, just pink enough in the middle to be juicy, but not so red that she envisioned dead cows.

Poor Kev always had found it easier to satisfy her with food.

"So if the marine biologists aren't the problem, why are you studying here rather than at your place? Is Davenport hassling you?"

The good thing about Smuggler's Cove was that it was small enough that everyone knew everybody. The bad thing about Smuggler's Cove was that everyone knew everybody else's business.

"Maddy?"

She tried to stem the red flush that climbed her jawline. "Yeah, Kev?"

"He's not bothering you, is he? You know, *bothering you?*"

Well, yeah Brody was bothering her, but not the way Kevin meant. Actually, she might be in a better frame of mind if the biologist *had* "bothered" her a little. "No. No, of course not. He's been a model guest. They all have."

"Well, if he tries anything, you just let me know."

Maddy assured Kevin that she would, although she had no intention of doing so. The gossip surrounding their failed engagement had just begun to die down and she felt no need to resurrect the topic by having her ex-fiancé beat up a guest.

She ate the rest of her burger while they talked of friendly things, but when Kevin walked with her to the boardwalk outside Mary Jo's he grew serious once again. He nodded to the red book under her arm.

"Do you ever think about it?"

She didn't pretend to misunderstand. "Sometimes. When the house is empty after a family with kids has stayed a while, I think about what it would have been like. You would have made a great daddy, Kev." She realized how that sounded and added, "You *will* make a great daddy. Just not with me."

He touched her arm when she would have turned and walked away. "Are you sure of that?"

Looking up into his gentle brown eyes, seeing the familiar lock of hair fall over his eye, Maddy concentrated on the feel of Kevin's hand on her arm. It felt like a hand. A warm, firm, capable hand—but a hand nonetheless. It didn't feel like grabbing onto lightning, or like touching a live wire, or even like zapping herself with static electricity. There was no spark. Zilch.

She shook her head with real regret. "I'm sure, Kev, and you're sure too. We've been there before and it didn't work. There's no reason to think it'd be any different this time."

He nodded. "Yeah, that's about what I figured. But promise me you'll be careful with this Davenport guy?"

"Of course."

Kevin bent and brushed a friendly kiss across her lips and she hugged him back before heading back to the Inn. As she crossed the boardwalk, she thought of her unsettling lodger and wondered.

Would she be able to get some work done if she just gave in and kissed him? Maybe it would be just as awkward an act as it had been with Kev. Maybe it would be wholly uninspiring. Maybe the only reason she was obsessing about Brody was because he was off limits.

Or maybe she was in deep, deep trouble.

Brody watched them from a parking space across the street. Ostensibly, he was scouting the local beaches for good viewing spots. He even had his camera along to record the fins and flukes of any coastal marine mammals he might chance to see. It was amazing the social patterns Violet could extrapolate from documenting the positions of herds, pods, groups, and subgroups over time, and part of the Smuggler's Cove Project would involve predicting those movements using computer simulation.

He'd already identified several pods of harbor porpoises and a mother humpback and calf that frequented the waters of Smuggler's Cove. He'd also seen a lone bottlenose with a scarred dorsal fin that reminded him of the female he'd saved off Provincetown just before he came to Smuggler's Cove.

He hoped it was the same dolphin, hoped the old girl had stayed afloat long enough for the stranding madness to clear from her brain.

But today, while the others readied the boat for the next series of experiments, he hadn't managed to photograph a single fluke, fin, or seal pup. In fact, he'd only seen the ocean a few times. Instead he'd found himself cruising the streets of Smuggler's Cove in search of his landlady.

Then he saw her come out of Mary Jo's diner. A big handsome man had his arm slung over her shoulders. The guy, with his perfectly mussed hair and fake-looking tan, kissed her as if he had every right to. And just like that, Brody's casual, I'm-taking-the-day-off-because-the-boat's-not-ready attitude vanished.

He wanted to run across the street, yank the big blond away from Maddy, and plant a fist right in the guy's perfect nose. He wanted to march over there, grab Maddy away from the animated Ken doll, and lay a kiss of his own on her, one that would immediately wipe out all traces of Ken's kiss and would forever supercede all other kisses in her memory.

He wanted to bang his head against the windshield of the Jeep until sanity returned.

What was it with Maddy Jamison? They'd barely even had a full conversation. Yet he was physically, elementally aware of her whenever she was in the house, and when she was gone, the emptiness echoed.

She was always in his thoughts, lurking at the

edges of his mind even as he watched a humpback calf breach in play. He could close his eyes and summon the memory of her scent. He wanted her like he had wanted no other woman before, and that was . . . well, impossible.

He couldn't afford to get caught up in something messy right now. He was counting on the Smuggler's Cove Project to get him noticed by the right people, so that when his grant came up for renewal the gigantic budget increase would be accepted and his plans for an international stranding research center would be approved.

The Smuggler's Cove Project would be a combination of the best new technologies along with a few older pieces of equipment like his beloved SSM. If they could use the data gathered in Smuggler's Cove to speed up rescue times and beef up survival statistics, then Brody would have congressional and senatorial support for the stranding center. Nothing was more important than that. Certainly not a woman he'd just met.

Maddy and the Ken doll finally broke their embrace. Ken returned to the diner and Brody wondered snidely whether he was the dishwasher or the bartender. Maddy crossed the street and turned toward the Inn, carrying a small stack of books.

Brody rolled up next to her and called through the open window, "Hey pretty lady, want a ride?"

She laughed because they were already at her driveway. "No thanks, it's not far." She quickened her steps and Brody had a feeling she was going to try to make it into the Inn before he was out of the Jeep. He had thought over the last couple of days that she had been quietly avoiding him. Now he was sure of it.

Undaunted, he stalled the engine, leaped out of the vehicle, and ran onto the porch so he was standing in front of the door, leaning against it with his arms folded over his chest when she reached him.

She stopped and eyed him warily. "Can I help you, Mr. Davenport?"

"I really think you should call me Brody. After all, I did rescue you from that man-eating fish, Dusty." When she stiffened, he glanced at the stack of books she was carrying, picked out a familiar cover, and whistled. "P-chem? That's pretty heavy stuff."

"For a girl?" She filled in the blank as though spoiling for a fight.

"Nah. For anyone. I hated physical chemistry almost as much as I hated organic, and that was a whole lot. It was just my bad luck the marine bio program required both of them. I made it through—barely—with the help of a lab tech named Fiona." He grinned. "Pretty Fiona . . ."

Maddy bet Fiona was about eight feet tall, willowy, brunette, and perfectly tanned. Everything she was not.

Brody seemed to recall himself to the present and asked, "Are you taking a course?"

She snorted. "No, I'm doing this for fun. Of course I'm taking a class. I've got a couple to make up before I go back to school."

Why had she told him that? But he didn't seem to find the idea funny at all. Instead he nodded as if he thought it a perfectly reasonable plan. "Cool. What're you going to study? I'm assuming it's grad school if p-chem's a requirement." He glared at the text as if half-afraid it was going to leap out of her arms and spew electrons at him.

"Nursing maybe. Or environmental studies. Or vet school." She shrugged and wished she'd made it into the house. Even standing on the porch next to Brody made her wish for foolish things. "I don't have a great plan yet. I've just barely admitted to myself that I want to go back." She didn't mention the two years of grad school already under her belt, nor the circumstances of her leaving Santa Cruz.

"Where'd you do your undergrad degree?" He paused. "No, let me guess." He squinted at her and put his fingertips to his forehead. "I'm getting the vibes of a snooty all-girls school in New England." He opened his eyes and suggested,

"Smith? Mount Holyoke? Ivy and brick buildings?"

She laughed, but had to wonder what about her made him think such a thing. "Way wrong," she told him. "Try again."

Humming agreeably, he passed a mystical hand in front of her face and she could feel heat rise in its wake. "I'm still getting brick and ivy. Radcliffe? No," he corrected himself. "You said I was way off, so it's not a girls' school. Dartmouth? No? How 'bout farther south—I've got it! Duke." He looked at her expectantly. "Right?"

She grinned. "Nope. Still way off. Like the totally wrong coast."

"California?" His voice almost squeaked in surprise.

"Yep, U.C. Santa Cruz." She nodded smugly.

"Hey! That's where I went for my doctorate." He looked pleased and Maddy could've kicked herself. Of course he'd gone to UCSC. It boasted one of the biggest and best marine mammal programs in the world. Where else would a dolphin biologist go?

She changed the subject before he could ask about graduation dates and mutual acquaintances. The last thing she wanted to do was reminisce. "Did you want something from me, or were you just headed home?" A patently ridiculous question, as he'd sprinted to beat her to the door.

"I was wondering if you'd like to walk with me tonight."

Maddy's heart sang quickly at the idea of walking with him in the sunset, talking of everything and nothing, but she knew it couldn't happen. "Where?"

He answered automatically, just as she had known he would, "Down by the beach, maybe out to the last jetty. It's pretty out there. Romantic."

Then he paused, as if hearing his own words. "Sorry. I guess we could head toward . . ." He trailed off when she smiled sadly.

"See? That's why it's not even worth trying, Brody. But thanks for the offer." And she slipped inside the Inn before he could see the moisture that gathered in her eyes.

Chapter Six

"We've hit the end of that grid, boss. You want me to swing her around and start the next lane?"

Brody grunted a reply and Smitty spun the wheel, keeping a careful eye on the cable connecting the SSM to the boat, making sure the umbilicus didn't get fouled in the reverse. Between the murk of the water and the speed *Streaker* was maintaining, Ahab wasn't going to see much through the submerged portholes, but both interns had taken to the semi-submersible and liked riding in it when there was nothing more pressing to be done.

They called it a cross between water-skiing and diving, and Ishmael had gone so far as to ask to

86

be dragged behind the Zodiac in his diving equipment so he could try it for real. He was promptly shouted down.

In reality, Brody was grateful for the diversion because there hadn't been much real action—of a personal or marine biological nature—in the weeks they'd been working around Smuggler's Cove.

They straggled back into port each night, grateful for the home-cooked meals and clean sheets Maddy provided, then set out again the next morning in hope of solid contact, but none had been forthcoming.

There had been a few humpbacks that flirted briefly with the boat before sounding with a flick of white-patterned flukes, and a cheerful band of harbor seals that barked *Streaker* to sea each day from their rookery on a small island at the mouth of the cove. But real, sustained interaction with either whales or dolphins had been sadly lacking.

That, Brody told himself, was the reason he looked forward to docking each night. It was the frustration of a fish finder screen bare of large contacts, the endless hours of scanning an empty sea for the distinctive V-shaped blow of the baleen whale, the frustratingly silent underwater microphones that ought to be squalling with dolphin catcalls and raspberries.

That was why he looked forward to coming

home at night. Not because Maddy was there, looking fresh as a morning breeze coming off Smuggler's Point. Looking utterly loveable.

And in the morning, when he left her in search of dolphins, if it took a few hours for the sea air to wash the smell of flowers and sunlight from his nostrils, nobody else needed to know of it. Because he and Maddy agreed there was no point in starting something that could only end badly.

"A hotbed of marine mammal populations? Hah." Violet slapped a sheaf of depth printouts against her leg as she came out of the sonar room and into the midmorning sun. "More like a big old ocean with a few practical jokers that like to play tag with our equipment."

With an irritated sigh, she sank to the deck next to Brody and leaned against the wheelhouse with her arm almost brushing his.

For some reason, her ill temper smoothed out his own a bit and he stretched his legs and crossed them at the ankles before waving at the limitless blue undulating before them. "But it's a lovely big ocean, isn't it? So the critters are playing hard to get? Well, we've done part of our job already with the underwater depth maps you've nearly finished, and the temperature readings the kids have put together. So when the whales and dolphins choose to oblige, we'll be more than ready for them."

"Thar she blows!"

Brody grinned and offered Violet a hand up. "See? What did I tell you? They're flocking to us already." He raised his voice in a hail, "Ishmael, what do you see?"

From the crow's nest above came Brody's favorite phrase in all the world. "*Tursiops,* sir!"

The bottlenose dolphins had arrived.

As usual, Maddy saved Brody's room for last. She worked calmly, efficiently smoothing his sheets the same as she did those of every other bed, plumping his pillows identically, tidying his room impersonally.

At least she tried to.

She couldn't help it if his scent rose up to fill her head with fantasies—improbable, impossible fantasies involving a dolphin biologist and an ocean-hating innkeeper. She snatched her hand away from his pillow, realizing that she had been stroking it unconsciously, much as she imagined touching his hair.

"Pitiful," she muttered. "Just pitiful. I should've married Kevin when I had the chance. Probably would have if I'd known what was coming. Right, Marmalade?"

But the cat wasn't there. He had taken to spending most of his time in Smitty's room, watching in fascination as the sucker fish progressed up the glass wall, bumped into the screen lid, and worked his way back down to the water again.

"Traitor," Maddy muttered, and glared out the window towards the ocean as if she could make *Streaker* appear just by wishing for it.

"See guys? I told you she was losing it. She's staring out the window and talking to herself. I think a ten-step program is called for."

Maddy spun around and was astounded to see Levi, Chrissy, Michael, and Kevin all clustered in the doorway of Brody's room, staring at her with identically comical worried looks.

"Step one." Kevin held up one of the baskets he used to transport his wonderful pastries. "Chocolate and butter, with enough dough to hold it all together and pretend it's a cookie."

"Step two." Michael brandished a bottle of Maddy's favorite wine and another of sparkling grape juice. "Alcohol so we can feel decadent for drinking at lunch, and enough other stuff so those of us that are pregnant," he slanted a look at his wife, "or not drinking can still indulge."

"Step three." Not to be outdone, Chrissy flapped a checkered blanket at her husband. "Protection for our precious backsides."

"And step four." Levi hefted an enormous picnic basket. "Enough of Kev's fine cooking to keep us away from our respective jobs for the rest of the afternoon."

Maddy grinned at the quartet, feeling like she hadn't seen them in years rather than the week or so that she'd been busy trying to concentrate on her p-chem exam while fending off wistful thoughts about the friendliest of the Dolphin Friendlies. She asked, "What're steps five through ten?"

Levi, always the ringleader, shrugged. "Something about admitting to your infatuation and calling on your higher power to combat it. Or pursue it, whichever works for you."

Kevin winced at the word *infatuation,* and Chrissy piped up, "And I'm pretty sure steps nine and ten refer to telling your best friends everything that's happened so far, and not censoring any of it, even the embarrassing parts."

Not surprisingly, Kev excused himself soon after that, touching Maddy's cheek softly as he passed and whispering, "Please be sure, Mads. I'd hate to see you hurt."

She stared after him for a moment, wishing she could have felt for him half of the crazy, impractical things she felt for the unattainable, untouchable master of Dolphin Friendly.

Levi cleared his throat and she realized the others were watching her.

"So? Do we have a picnic?" Chrissy's eyes

pleaded with Maddy in that undeniable way only pregnant best friends can manage. "We've missed you."

Maddy thought of the mountainous pile of laundry awaiting her downstairs, of the Cajun chicken she was planning as a surprise for Smitty, and of the grad school applications lurking in her desk—papers that contained such questions as "If you could be a tree, what kind of a tree would you be and why?" and "How have your life experiences prepared you for the rigors of graduate-level course work?"

Then she looked at the expectant faces of her friends and out the window to the beautiful day beyond and decided, *What the heck? All that stuff will be here when I get back.*

"You're on. Where are we going?" Usually they picnicked on the common or in the pretty garden behind town hall, but Maddy was suddenly itchy for a new view. A new challenge.

"It's your picnic, you choose," urged Levi, and the others nodded in agreement.

Maddy inhaled a deep breath and took what felt like the biggest plunge of her life.

"Let's eat on the beach."

The dolphins stayed near *Streaker* for an hour, playing and calling to one another like boys on a schoolyard basketball court.

Violet shot miles of film, focusing on the acrobatic jumps that left the animal's entire body out of the water for seconds at a time. She called everyone's attention to the lighter scrapes and scars decorating the dark-gray skin of each dolphin.

"Did you see that one?" she asked Brody, grinning as they watched a young calf taunt the grizzled matriarch of the bunch. "The big old female? She's led a hard life."

Brody nodded. "Yeah, from the slashes on her back, I'd say she's run afoul of more than one motorboat in her life. In fact, she's probably lucky to be alive. See how stiffly she swims?" He pointed when the dolphin in question obliged the youngster by chasing it a short distance away, then shepherding it back to the group.

"Takes a lickin' and keeps on tickin', eh boss?" Smitty joined them and Violet scowled at him and walked away. "Hey, what'd I say?"

"Nothing. You never do," she snapped over her shoulder before lifting the vidcam again and training it on a trio of young adults that were frolicking around Ahab and the SSM.

Ignoring his friends' bickering—which seemed to have grown more common of late—Brody watched the old female and tried to decide whether she was the same dolphin he'd pushed back to sea a few weeks earlier. When she rolled over and floated on her back for a few seconds, he was sure of it. Her belly bore a series of scoured patches that were almost healed—a sure sign of stranding.

Pleased that she'd lived to rejoin her band, and wondering why she'd left it in the first place, he cocked his head at Smitty. "You and Violet have a fight?"

"When aren't we fighting?" A pensive look crept into his eyes. "Face it, boss. The two of us haven't gotten along great since we all graduated."

Startled, Brody thought back and tried to find a time in memory that Smitty and Violet hadn't fought. It seemed to him it'd always been that way . . . except. "That's true. You guys were pretty close in school, before you married—"

He broke off and stared. A vein in Smitty's jaw pulsed.

"Let it lie, boss," he said in an even voice. "It's ancient history."

Brody would've stuttered out an incoherent question, but was interrupted by the cry from above.

"Thar she blows!"

Brody wasn't sure who was more relieved, he

or Smitty. He called, "What do you see, Ish-mael?"

"*Mus musculus,* sir!"

"I really wish the kid didn't insist on calling everything by its taxonomic name," Smitty grumped. "I haven't had to think about Latin in forever." Then he snickered. "Is *Mus musculus* what I think it is?"

Grinning, Brody nodded. "Our daredevil spotter has sighted the fearsome—" He paused dramatically and they said it together.

"Field mouse!"

"Ishmael," Brody shouted at the crow's nest, "get it right or don't bother trying to be smarter than us old folks. Assuming you didn't sight an enormous, amphibious rodent, tell us what you do see."

"Uh, *Megaptera novaeangliae,* sir."

"Ishmael." Brody's growl was a warning. How quickly the kid's respectful awe had worn off. But that was okay. If Ishmael ever got over feeling like he was the smartest person in the room, he'd make a fine researcher.

"Just kidding. Humpbacks, sir. Feeding about a half mile out."

"Thank you, Ishmael."

Brody took the wheel himself and grinned when the dolphins fell into formation, riding

Streaker's bow like glistening gray children, squealing excitedly when their humpback cousins came into sonar range.

As if in greeting, a hoary old male exploded into the air, his broad flukes propelling most of his sixty tons out of the water before the behemoth rolled to his back and crashed into the sea in the most spectacular breach Brody had ever seen. The humpback's flippers, fifteen feet long if they were an inch, waved grandly in the air as the animal sank amidst a glittering shower.

Brody could barely swallow past the lump in his throat.

Another whale breached, a juvenile male who corkscrewed all the way around and flicked his white-frosted flukes out of the water as he landed. The crew of Dolphin Friendly applauded and the dolphins chattered and leapt in the froth.

The humans on the boat oohed and aahed at each leap and Brody was reminded of families watching a fireworks display. He wondered whether Smuggler's Cove had a Fourth of July celebration, whether Maddy liked to attend. Whether she would go with him if he promised not to talk about the ocean.

He imagined she would wear one of those flowing sundresses he'd seen her in from time to time. He pictured her lying beside him on a checkered blanket, her eyes shining in the reflected pyrotechnics, her lips pouted just so.

And Brody suddenly felt as though she was standing at his shoulder, watching the show.

Two humpbacks detonated out of the ocean at the same time and arched toward each other, looking as if one must certainly land on the other. But through a miracle, or by a sort of three-dimensional spatial planning that humans had yet to understand, the whales passed each other by mere feet, landing in the water with enormous dual splashes just as a trio of dolphins leaped straight up and spun madly in the rising plumes of water.

A filmmaker couldn't have choreographed it better.

Brody turned to the imagined woman beside him, wanting to see his own excitement reflected in her eyes, needing to share the awesome, precious beauty with her.

She wasn't there. Of course she wasn't.

A wave of disappointment rolled over him and he stared sightlessly back toward land. The glitter left the waves, the dolphin's cries dulled slightly, and each of the five humpbacks took several deep breaths and rolled to dive, white and black flukes pointing straight into the air as they descended to depths that man had only recently plumbed.

"Boss?"

Brody started, having not realized Smitty was at his elbow. He wondered how long his assistant had been standing there. "Yeah?" His voice sounded gritty even to him.

"What do you want to do?"

The whales were gone, the dolphins dispersing. It was time to head for shore. But just as Brody was about to give the order to reel in the microphones and lock the equipment down for the night, a rolling bell of sound erupted from the sonar room as Violet turned up the gain on the underwater acoustics.

It started down low, at a frequency that left the metal sides of the *Streaker* humming and pulsing, then ascended like a badly tuned cello before dropping again below the ken of human hearing. A second voice joined the first, sobbing in an alien harmony.

The whales were singing.

Brody saw the awe on the faces around him, the shining joy of contact, of experience. There had been days that he and Smitty and Violet had sat for three, four, even ten hours at a stretch and listened to the otherworldly concert of singing humpbacks. He saw that need in them now, the love of the joy and beauty that each of them found in the ocean.

And he felt itchy. Twitchy.

The song rose and fell around them, dutifully recorded in the sonar room by their digital systems. But no reproduction could ever come close to the experience.

One of the underwater voices slid into a higher register, a scratchy descant that got under Brody's skin and crawled there like an impulse. An urge.

"Boss?" Smitty held out a diver's octopus, an awkward collection of metal and tubing that bolted to the air tank and fed the regulator and buoyancy compensating vest. "What do you want to do?"

The group often dived with singing whales— not necessarily down to the level where the behemoths hung slightly head down with their flippers held away from their sides as they sang, but far enough into the ocean to slide beneath the restless waves and be surrounded by the throbbing vibrations of whalesong. It was the ultimate experience. An unbelievable high.

"You go ahead," Brody told him, waving to include the rest of Dolphin Friendly. "Pairs only, forty minutes each, no deeper than thirty feet so you won't need to decompress, and keep it safe, okay?"

"What are you going to do?"

Brody grabbed a navy blue windbreaker that

said *Stranding Rescue* in three-inch letters across the back, and slid down the ladder to where one of the Zodaics bobbed obediently next to the boat. "I'm going home."

Chapter Seven

Maddy was in the kitchen perfecting Cajun seasoning for Smitty's surprise when the front door opened and she heard footsteps headed up the stairs. Startled, she glanced out toward the dock. She hadn't heard the distinctive chug of *Streaker*'s engines returning her to port. Sure enough, the research vessel was nowhere in sight.

A Zodiac was tied at Big Jim's Pier. Was there something wrong with the boat? A shiver of unease coursed through her at the thought, a memory best left unremembered, of another time, another boat.

Another captain.

She abandoned her chicken and hurried to the stairs, pausing on the first step as Brody emerged

101

from his bedroom. He had a towel looped around his neck and was wearing only jeans, his chest and feet bare for the walk to the shower.

Maddy froze. Memory had paled a bit in the almost three weeks since his arrival. Since then, she had seen very little of the body she'd once seen in a wetsuit, and had almost convinced herself that he wasn't as well-built as she remembered.

But he was all that and more. And he was staring down at her as if mesmerized, a strange light burning deep within his murky eyes. In another man she might have called that light desire, but with Brody that was too plain an emotion. They might want each other as man and woman, but the differences between them made a simple feeling incredibly complex.

Yet the way he was looking at her, with an intensity that seemed to strip away her clothing and her flesh all at once and stare down into her very heart, made her think that something had happened to upset Brody's carefully developed equilibrium, had made him decide darn the complications, darn her fears and his work and all the things that stood between them.

"Brody? Is something wrong?" She'd meant to ask about *Streaker,* but it didn't come out that way.

He snorted mirthlessly. "Wrong? Nothing's

wrong. Or everything's wrong depending on how you look at it." He rubbed the towel back and forth across his neck and his muscles shimmered just under the warm, tan skin.

"Where are the others? Is something wrong with your boat?"

"The others? They're still out on the water listening to the whales sing. Why am I here? Because I couldn't concentrate. I needed to see you."

He descended a few steps until he was just one tread above her. She could smell the salt spray on his body, the faint taint of the ocean that she so despised.

"Did you hear what I said? I left dolphins for you. Singing whales. For you." He looped the towel over her neck and used it to bring her face closer to his. "I've never done anything like that before. Ever."

Just when she thought it was inevitable that he finally kiss her, Brody released the towel and leaned back. "I'm going to take a shower." He turned and jogged back up the stairs, leaving Maddy standing, dumbfounded. At the top, Brody turned and looked down at her, that strange light burning even brighter in his eyes. "And Maddy?"

"Yes?"

"The others will be late for dinner. Will you walk with me?"

He'd asked her to walk with him before, always down to the sea. Though she had survived her picnic, secure in the support of her friends, Maddy couldn't bear it again that day. So she asked, "Where?"

Brody shrugged. "Wherever you want, Princess."

I'm not primping, Maddy assured herself as she fluffed her hair with her fingers and squinted into the bedroom mirror, trying to decide whether to slap on some lipstick or not. *Well,* she allowed as she recapped the tube of Passion Pink and touched some perfume to her wrists and ears, *maybe I'm primping a little.*

"But I'm absolutely not changing," she told Marmalade, who purred and kneaded the bedspread in response.

She was sure Brody would notice it if she traded the old jeans and soft yellow shirt for something more . . . appealing. Like three-inch heels and a leather miniskirt, neither of which she owned but could probably borrow from Levi. She remembered him wearing something of the sort to the Halloween Dance last year.

He'd looked darned good, too, but in retrospect Maddy had to allow that the outfit probably wasn't appropriate for an evening walk.

So she fluffed her hair one last time and turned

for the door just as she heard Brody's steps on the stairs. "Maddy? Are you ready to go?"

Then she noticed the stain on her shirt, a spot of paprika, pepper, and oil on the material near her collar. A splash of the sauce she'd used for Smitty's Cajun chicken must have gotten past her apron. Darn. She was going to have to change after all. Should she wear the silk blouse she'd bought for Chrissy and Michael's Christmas party last year, or the strappy halter top she'd not found occasion to wear yet?

"Maddy?"

She snorted at herself. Brody wouldn't care what she wore unless it was a wetsuit. Besides, they were going for a walk through town, not down the aisle.

And where had *that* thought come from?

"Oh, never mind," she grumbled at Marmalade, who smiled a smug feline grin as Maddy left the bedroom and sailed out into the hallway.

"I'm ready!"

That was a bit of an overstatement, Brody soon realized as he spent the next five minutes watching her flit around the Inn, turning off an excellent-smelling dinner, setting the table, and leaving a note to the crew, telling them to help themselves if they got back before she did.

Brody could've told her not to bother. He'd be

surprised to see Dolphin Friendly before the next day, but he didn't tell Maddy that—it might make her more nervous.

But as he watched her buzz through the hall for the tenth time and felt his own stomach flutter slightly, it occurred to him. *He* was nervous. Which was silly; they'd been living in the same house for several weeks. Nothing was different.

Everything was different.

So he caught her arm on her next flyby and made her stop, felt her pulse thrumming beneath his thumb. "Hey, Princess. It's just a walk, okay? Let's go."

They stared at each other a beat, almost nose to nose until she pulled free from his hold and nodded.

"You're right of course. I don't know what's . . . never mind. Let's go."

He walked at her side through town, close but not touching, and he imagined he could feel the warmth of her body all through his own. He let her lead, figuring she would choose a road that led away from the beach, and was startled when she guided him to a path that followed the line of the dunes. They stayed on the land side of the sand hillocks, where the beach met solid ground, the trail a compromise between earth and sea.

Brody smiled ironically. That's what he and

Maddy needed. A place where her life and his could intersect. Neutral territory.

They walked in silence and he felt himself begin to relax, lulled by the sound of the waves hissing on the shore just a few hundred feet away. He'd meant to ask her about her fear of the sea, planned to find out whether there was any chance she could ever overcome her aversion and join him, even once in a while, on *Streaker*. Because he'd needed her there today.

But when he spoke, he surprised himself by asking, "What about the Ken doll?"

When that was met with an appropriately baffled silence, he forged on. "The guy at Mary Jo's Diner. I saw you kiss him. Is he—are you and he . . . ?"

"Oh. Kevin." She walked in silence for several more steps and Brody felt his own tension rise. While he had no aversion to a little healthy competition, he wasn't about to upset an existing relationship just because he thought highly of a woman. Dreamed about her. Turned to talk to her when she wasn't there.

Then she answered him, reassured him. "We aren't together. Not anymore. Haven't been for a long time."

"But you were once?"

She nodded and stumbled a little as the shifting sand gave way. Brody took her arm to steady her and didn't let go once they were on more solid ground.

"We were engaged."

He suppressed the wince. Smitty had tried to tell him she was the marrying kind, the kind who wanted orange blossoms and picket fences and kids and the whole barrel of fish, but here was the proof. She wasn't the sort for a quick fling, or even a long one, with a man who was away from land as much as he was on it. And if she wouldn't come to sea with him . . .

It didn't leave much middle ground.

"Have you ever been married?" she asked him.

Dusk was creeping into the sky now, a little darkness at the edge of vision, a splash of snapper red and salmon pink at the horizon. It seemed as if her question came from those rays of color. He shook his head, knowing she could still see his profile well enough to read the action. "Never. Not too many women think of marine field biologists as a good bet for a family man."

Maddy flinched. He looked at her sharply. "What?"

"Nothing. It's that my . . . my friend's parents were researchers. They spent a lot of time away from their children."

"That happens sometimes, but it's a choice," Brody said. He'd met more than a few couples who kept their kids with them and made compromises that allowed the family to stay near good schools and the children's friends. "There are ways around that sort of thing." He wasn't sure why he was bothering to defend the profession to her. They certainly weren't going to marry. Have children.

Brody had a sudden image of Maddy helping a pair of squirming kids don pint-sized snorkeling equipment while *Streaker* bobbed lazily in tropical waters teeming with spinner dolphins and their spotted cousins.

He shook the image away and realized she was speaking.

"You and your crew are close."

He wasn't sure if she was changing the subject or just taking it on a tangent, but answered the question he thought she might be asking. "Violet and I aren't. Not anymore, at least not that way."

"I know." She tightened her grip and he wondered when his hand had slid down her arm and they had linked fingers. "She and Smitty can't decide whether to kill each other or love each other."

How was it that Maddy had seen in a few weeks what he hadn't in ten years? "I didn't know until today that they had . . ." He squirmed. "I never would have . . . If I had known . . . you know. Anyway, things between Violet and I ended a while ago. There just wasn't much of a spark."

"I know how that is." In the almost-dark, her voice sounded sad. Wistful.

"You and Ken?"

"Kevin. Yes." They walked in companionable silence until they came to a place where the dunes fell away and the path continued down to the ocean. She stopped and faced him.

She was looking toward the land, he toward the sea.

"This is an awkward place for us to find a spark, isn't it?"

He agreed with a nod. "Awkward, but not impossible."

"You're leaving in a few days?"

With a start, Brody realized it was true. The three weeks they had originally booked were almost at an end. The preliminary depth, temperature, and density readings were complete, and much of the weather and population information would be culled from other sources. Pretty soon they would be hunkered down with their computers, trying to make it into a simulation, a model they could use to beg for funding for the permanent research station.

"Well, if it was all right with you, I was thinking we might extend our stay." Subconsciously, he realized he had been thinking that since the moment she opened the door of the Inn. They could do their computing from Smuggler's Cove. It wasn't much more expensive than the apartments they rented month to month when they were on shore duty, and laundry and food were included. None of the gang would complain.

She inhaled deeply as if considering the possibility. "I'm not sure that would be a good idea."

"Why? Because of what I am?" He cursed softly when she continued to stare over his shoulder, away from the sea. "It's not like I'm an axe murderer, Princess. So what if I like fish and you don't? We can work around that."

"It's not that, Brody. It's . . ." She looked at him with fear in her eyes. Real fear. He stepped toward her and she retreated. "It's not safe out there. People die."

Brody found a glimmer of understanding. "Your friend's parents?" She nodded, although he sensed it wasn't the whole truth.

"They died doing field work. On the water. So I watch every day for your boat to come home, knowing that someday it won't. I can't live like that." She glanced up at him. "I won't live like that."

"But things are safer now, Princess," he tried to reassure her even as a warm glow worked its way through him. She was worried about him. She cared about him. This shouldn't be an impossible dream. "We have GPS tracking systems, homing devices, better weather prediction, all sorts of things designed to keep us safe."

He took a step toward her and this time she didn't back away, whether because the sand was beginning to crumble beneath her, or because she welcomed his nearness, Brody wasn't sure. He reached out and traced his thumb across her bottom lip. "If I tell you I'm coming home, Princess, I promise I won't let you down."

"But what if you can't?" she barely whispered.

"I will." And he brought his lips down to hers, savoring that first contact before deepening the kiss.

She answered in kind, reaching up to wrap her arms around his neck and anchor his mouth to hers.

The red light bled from the sky to be replaced with blue-black darkness lit only by a tiny sliver of moon. The few houses along the dunes came to life like the running lights of a small yacht.

Through it all, Brody held his woman in his arms. And wished.

They didn't speak as they walked hand-in-hand back to the Inn, and Brody was glad for the silence because it gave him time to think. She was afraid for him, and he had promised to be careful. But he knew better than most that things happened out on the water, things that couldn't be predicted, couldn't be controlled. What right did he have to blithely swear that he'd come back safe from every run?

And what had happened to her to need that promise? That story about her friend's parents was at least partly true, but he had a feeling the association was closer. A lover? A family member?

Something niggled at the back of his brain. She'd mentioned a brother once in passing. His name was Mark or something. Mark Jamison. Why did that sound familiar?

They reached the Inn, the return seeming much quicker than the journey. Brody dallied on the front porch while Maddy entered and, as was her habit, checked the answering machine first.

"Boss?" Smitty's voice was tinny, scratchy with distance, wind, and a bad cell phone connection. They'd probably run the boat near shore just to get that much of a cell and Brody appreciated the effort. "Just wanted to let you know we're staying out here for the night. The dolphins are back and Violet and the interns are naming them for our records. The big scarred female is 'Mother' and that juvenile who mimics all the adults we're calling 'Ditto.' There are a couple of long-finned pilot whales and Ahab swears he saw a right whale mother and calf blow about a half mile out to port, but I told him that rights are about as common in the Atlantic as unicorns in Manhattan."

There was the sound of a scuffle and Violet's voice came on the line. "Brody? If you're coming out, call on the little radio and we'll pick you up somewhere. Otherwise we'll meet you on the dock in the morning about eight, okay? Gotta go." And the line went dead, hissing emptily until the answering machine beeped to indicate no more messages.

A curious detachment came over Brody, a sudden split in his life. The one part of him, a part he was dimly aware of but couldn't quite connect to the rest of him, said *Wow! Right whale! There aren't more than a few hundred left in the North Atlantic. And a calf? I've got to get out there!*

But the rest of him stared at Maddy as she stood in the downstairs hallway looking at him with a gentle question in her eyes.

"Are you going back out?"

Was he going back to *Streaker*? He should. There was stuff happening out on the water without him and he ought to be there, needed to be directing the crew and educating the interns. That was his job. His life.

But he didn't want to. He wanted to stay.

"Brody?"

He held her eyes, shrugged. "That depends."

"On what?"

"On what you want me to do. What do you want, Maddy?"

Her color rose higher and she touched a finger to her lips. Then she held a hand out to him and saved them both, doomed them both, with a single word.

"Stay."

Chapter Eight

"I don't know what's wrong with me." Maddy sank her head into her hands the next morning. "It's like the sensible, practical Maddy is now sharing space in my head with this deranged floozy who doesn't care for an instant that Brody Davenport is . . . well, what he is."

"Cool!" Christine grabbed another of the warm chocolate-chip cookies Levi had brought from Mary Jo's. "Yum. Kev must've known you'd need help today. He baked."

Maddy lifted her head enough to glare at Levi, who mimed his innocence and pointed back at Chrissy. "This isn't funny, you two. Why?" she practically wailed, trying not to remember what a nice dinner she and Brody had shared the night before, just the two of them and six people's worth of Cajun chicken. "Why couldn't I have drooled over Kevin half as much as this guy?"

If she had, she'd be safely married to a lifetime supply of chocolate-chip cookies.

"But nooo," she mocked herself. "I had to hold out for a man who really interested me. I couldn't be satisfied with good old Kev—I wanted to wait for excitement."

"Excitement's good," Levi chimed in brightly, earning himself another glare from Maddy, who plowed on.

"And so I wait another couple of years—date-less years—practically living like a hermit while I wait for an interesting man—and what happens? A guy comes along and presses each and every one of the buttons Kevin never did."

She appealed to her friends, who watched in rapt fascination. "He's beautiful, for Pete's sake— you said so yourself, right, Chris?"

Christine nodded. "Almost a sculpture," she added helpfully. "We could call him 'Wetsuited Man on the Halfshell,' or something."

Maddy nodded, knowing that the new anti-Maddy had taken control of her brain and not really caring. "Absolutely. He's lean and has all these interesting muscles, he's hairy in all the right places, and . . ." She dropped her head back into her hands and clenched her fingers in her hair.

"What was the point I was about to make? I was going to say that—"

The other two chimed in to make a three-part harmony, "He's a marine biologist!"

Maddy tried to wither them with a look, but neither Chrissy nor Levi looked particularly repentant. She grumbled, "You guys weren't in Smuggler's Cove yet when my parents died. You didn't see how it was, how the press kept it going for months afterward, how it practically killed Nana and Grampie every time they saw that tape on the news."

"But Mads, this guy wasn't there. He has nothing to do with what happened." Chrissy laid a gentle hand on Maddy's forearm and Levi nodded in agreement.

"That's not it," said Maddy glumly. "It's not just that he's a marine biologist. For heaven's sake, my brother's one and I don't hate him." At least not anymore. "It's that Brody's like our father was, and for men like that it's not just a job. It's a whole way of living life that I don't want. Not again."

When neither of her friends had an answer for that, Maddy took her leave—and the remaining cookies—and headed back to the Inn.

The house felt empty when she got home.

Empty and alone. Or perhaps, thought Maddy, she was projecting her own feelings on an inanimate pile of lumber and hardware.

Either way, where once she would have found the solitude a welcome relief, now she felt lonely, irritated with the endless round of chores and dreading the necessary call to the plumber for her ailing washing machine, which had eaten everyone's underwear the day before. Even cleaning Brody's room brought her no peace, for in it she found a thousand reminders of him, of their dinner the night before, and of the fact that he would only be there a short time longer.

How could she have let this happen?

"I'm an idiot, aren't I, Marmalade? There isn't a human being on this planet more wrong for me than Brody Davenport, is there?"

There was no response. No purr, no meep, no sarcastic meow. Nothing.

"Marmalade?"

Curious, Maddy poked her head into Violet's room, then into the one shared by the two interns. No orange tabby cat. He was probably in Smitty's room, watching the suckerfish again.

Smitty's room was empty. No cat on the bed watching that ugly disk of flesh suck its way up the side of the tank and bump into the mesh lid. *Wait!* Maddy froze as her eyes registered what her brain was trying to tell her.

The lid was on the floor beside the tank.

The fish was gone.

Maddy hurried to the bedside table and dropped to her knees, frantically searching the floor while calling, "Dusty? Dusty!"

Stupid, she chided herself. *Fish don't come when you call them. Cats don't even come when you call them.* The only creatures that regularly responded to their names were dogs and occasionally men, especially when bribed with food.

"Grrrr."

Maddy paused. Had she really heard that? Did suckerfish growl? She didn't think so, but she scrunched so she could look under Smitty's bed, half afraid of what she would find down there.

A pair of boxers that had avoided the genocide recently perpetrated by her washing machine. A bit of dust that had escaped her weekly vacuuming raid. And a growling orange tabby cat with a dead-looking fish in its mouth.

"Marmalade! Drop it!"

Once again demonstrating the difference between cats and dogs, Marmalade flattened his ears against his skull and growled, challenging her to come and get his hard-won prey if she dared.

Maddy dared, all right. She stuck her hand under the bed and made a grab for the fish, earning a swat from the cat. Marmalade then reversed direction, shot out from under the bed, and bolted with Smitty's beloved pet in his mouth, swinging limply from side to side with every leap.

Maddy chased after, hollering for all she was worth in the hopes the cat would drop its captive. But Marmalade galloped down the stairs and headed for the open front door, claws scrabbling madly on the polished wood of the entryway.

"Nooo!"

The cat gained the clamshell driveway and accelerated across the road right in front of a hot-pink VW Beetle, which slammed on its brakes to avoid a collision. Levi stuck his head through the open driver's window. "Maddy? What's wrong?"

She yelled, "Catch that cat!" as she sailed in front of the Beetle and towards the Smuggler's Cove town common in hot pursuit of her soon-to-be-ex-pet.

Whooping, Levi abandoned his car in the road and joined the chase, soon followed by Chrissy, Michael and Kevin, who had been alerted that a game was afoot by Levi's Rebel yells.

Poor Marmalade, suddenly besieged from all sides by insanely yodeling humans, did the only sensible thing and shot straight up the big maple tree in front of the Smuggler's Cove Library.

The humans gathered around the fat trunk and gazed up, up, and up still, to the highest branches, where the orange cat crouched and glowered down at them with Dusty in his mouth.

"What's he got, one of Miss Minnie's hamsters?"

The local kindergarten teacher was fanatical about her hamsters, which she used to demonstrate "the wonders of Mother Nature" to her students. Many a Smuggler's Cove home was populated with one or more of Miss Minnie's offerings.

Maddy shook her head. "Nope. It belongs to one of my guests."

"The guest that gave you that hickey on your neck?"

She glared at Levi but didn't bother wincing. Kevin cringed hard enough for both of them. "No. Dusty belongs to the other one. Smitty."

Chrissy chimed in, "The redhead? He's kind of cute too, in a geeky sort of way." When Michael frowned, she bristled. "What? I don't have eyes in my head now that I'm pregnant?"

Thankfully, Levi redirected the conversation to the treed animals. "So what is it? A mouse?"

"A fish."

Her four friends, plus a few more inhabitants of Smuggler's Cove, turned to stare at Maddy as if she'd gone completely off her rocker.

"There's a fish in the tree?" asked one.

She nodded. "Yep. Sometimes he sort of sucks his way up the side of the tank and falls on the floor and you have to spray him with this stuff and put him back in the water and he swims away . . ." She trailed off as her friends continued to stare.

"You have a fish living with you?" To Levi, that fact was obviously more surprising than the fact that said fish was dangling forty feet or so off the ground.

"Um. Yes."

Oblivious to the drama, one of the waitresses from Mary Jo's suggested, "We could try throwing something at the cat and see if it'll drop the fish."

"And then what?" asked Michael. "If the fish is still alive, the fall will kill him. I think. I don't have much experience with flying fish."

"Well, we could stretch a towel or something down here, like a trampoline for it to fall on," Chrissy suggested, and was duly dispatched for a sheet or a large towel. She returned with both, along with a Chinese-style gong that Maddy remembered using at the Smuggler's Cove Talent Show one year.

"I thought instead of throwing anything at poor Marmalade, we could try to make lots of noise."

Michael, Chrissy, Levi, and Kevin all took corners of the sheet and stretched it tight. Leading with the gong, Maddy and the others then proceeded to make more than enough noise to wake a roomful of corpses.

It worked like a charm. In shock, amusement, or general annoyance, Marmalade dropped the fish and quit the field of battle. He jumped from a branch to the gutter of the library and picked his way down to the ground from there. He then strolled nonchalantly back to the Inn in search of his dinner, but nobody was watching him.

They were all staring at Dusty, who was stuck in a bird's nest about twenty feet above the ground.

"You know I hate it when you do this," Smitty groused as he handed his boss the weight belt that, in conjunction with the buoyancy compensator, would allow Brody to maintain a steady depth without effort. "I don't get how you can preach safety at the interns and then do this. Let me come with you. It's just not safe to dive without a buddy and you know it, not that that's ever stopped you before."

"You've just made your own point." Brody spit in his mask and rinsed it out to keep the glass from fogging underwater where it was tricky to fix. "I've been doing it for years and nothing's ever happened to me, right?" He grinned. "I'll be careful, Mom, I promise."

He just needed some time alone. As fond as he was of Dolphin Friendly, there were times the boat felt more than a little crowded. And as much as he—liked? loved? wanted? yes, wanted Maddy, he was in dire need of a few minutes to himself to try and sort through some of what he was feeling.

Diving was the best kind of alone he could ever imagine. And yes, technically it was dangerous to dive solo, but he checked and double-checked his equipment every time and strictly forbade any of the other team members to dive alone.

Brody reasoned that he didn't smoke and he didn't drink much, he didn't sleep around and he didn't drive like a maniac. A man was entitled to one vice, wasn't he?

Diving alone was his.

Smitty helped him buckle the heavy tanks in place and ran him through the predive checklist once more, just to be certain.

"I'll be fine. Smitty. I promised Maddy I'd come home tonight and take her out to dinner." But his promise hadn't quite erased the worry in her eyes. "If you want to head in early, just leave the Zodiac anchored over my flag so I don't have to swim to shore."

"Sure thing, boss. I might just do that." But they both knew *Streaker* would be waiting when Brody resurfaced.

He clamped the regulator between his teeth and savored the familiar taste of compressed oxygen and nitrogen and the drag of equipment that felt bulky on land but fell away to nothing in the water. Sketching a jaunty wave at his crew, he took a big step off *Streaker*'s deck and plummeted fins first into the Atlantic.

Instantly, he was in another world, an alien environment that ended above his head at the solid-seeming interface between air and water, and extended down beneath him to endless depths that the sonar claimed was only twenty feet or so but could have been miles.

The water was cold and he gritted his teeth until the thin layer of wet between his skin and the neoprene suit was warmed to a tolerable level by body heat. Then he checked his wrist computer, vented his BC to give him negative buoyancy, and headed for the bottom.

He heard only the burble of his own breath being inhaled from the tanks and released from the regulator in a glistening stream of silvery bubbles.

The waters off Cape Cod lacked the brilliant coral formations that attracted divers to other places, and overall the fish tended toward uninteresting grays and browns, but Brody had not entered this world as a sightseer. He had come to think.

So he adjusted his BC to counteract the weight

belt and achieved neutral buoyancy, hanging a few feet above the sea floor. He rolled onto his back and crossed his arms over his chest. *Streaker* seemed so far away, and Maddy even farther than that, much to his chagrin.

She would never dive with him. He would never be able to show her the reefs off St. John, never see her eyes light up at the sight of a striped clownfish hiding in an anemone's poisonous fronds.

She would never know the simple joy of swimming with dolphins.

Could he live with that?

Brody drifted, using an occasional flipper flick to keep him within sight of his boat. He remembered his own parents' bafflement with his driving need for the sea. How had the seemingly shiftless son of a hardscrabble cattle rancher become a successful dolphin biologist? It had always been, and would always remain a mystery to them.

The day he left for UCSC on a full scholarship, his mother had waved good-bye with a worried look in her eyes, the same look that Smitty's wife had worn each time she saw him off at the dock. Each time she had waved him home.

Promise me you'll come back, Maddy had asked with that look in her eyes, only ten times worse. Could he live with that pressure? That need?

Brody closed his eyes and tasted compressed air and the rubber of his regulator. He thought of Maddy and the cold water grew balmy. He smelled flowers and warm, dry sunlight. He felt her touch on his face, imagined her lips on his.

And he smiled as it came to him that the question wasn't whether he could live with her.

It was whether he could live without her—and the answer was no. One way or another, he had to make it work.

He opened his eyes and began to swim back to *Streaker,* only then becoming aware that he was surrounded by dolphins. They swam silently, slowly around him, maybe ten or twelve bottle-noses of various ages. One by one, they swam past him—close enough for him to reach out and touch a flipper, a fluke.

The last to make contact was Mother, the old female he had saved from stranding—was it only a few weeks ago? She hovered near him, needing neither BC nor weight belt to achieve perfect neutral buoyancy. He stroked her melon, the domed forehead in front of her blowhole where a series of air-filled sinuses created the sounds that made up dolphin language and echolocation.

I think that I love Maddy, he whispered inside

his head, wishing he could have said the words right then.

And he could have sworn the old dolphin smiled.

Chapter Nine

"**I** can't believe I fell out of the tree," Levi moaned, holding the icepack to his forehead and slouching back against the headboard of Smitty's bed.

"It wasn't quite a fall." Chrissy patted his hand. "You were far more graceful than that. I'd call it more of a swan dive that ended with a sudden, grassy impact."

"Gee thanks."

Maddy aimed the Better Butter at the motionless lump in her hand. "At least it was for a good cause. If what Smitty said before is true, then Dusty should still be alive. I'm sure he appreciates your heroic sacrifice."

At least she hoped the stupid fish did. She

hoped it was still alive, a state she couldn't quite determine since it almost always looked dead to her, even when it was sucking away at the side of the tank.

She wondered what Smitty saw in the ugly thing. But then again, he obviously saw some good in Violet as well, which is more than Maddy could claim.

"I should just fry you up," she told the greasy brown lump. "Stick you in a cast iron skillet and serve you for dinner."

"Maddy? Are you talking to that fish?"

She noticed that her friends were looking at her as if she had gone far, far off the deep end. "Uh."

Levi sat up, his mortal injuries forgotten. "Because if you are, I think it calls for a celebration, don't you? Think of it." He paused while she dropped Dusty back into his tank. "Think of it, you actually saved a fish's life today. You terrorized your own cat to save the existence of something you've hated for as long as Chrissy and I have known you."

From the foot of the bed, Marmalade glared at Maddy as if to say, *Yeah, what gives?*

Stalling, she checked the tank for signs of life. Dusty lay at the bottom, motionless. Potentially no longer of this world. What on earth was she going to tell Smitty?

"Maddy?"

She shrugged. "Well, Nana always said that I should do everything in my power to keep guests happy. Smitty's a guest and so is Dusty."

"Keeping guests happy. Is that what you're doing with Davenport?"

"Shut up, Levi."

Chrissy piped up, "No, I think he has a point. About the fish, not Brody—although I want to hear all about that later. You're allowing fish in the house. You took us to the beach yesterday for lunch. And you're going out to dinner with Brody tonight, which is a big step, don't you think? An actual date! I think this is really important, Mads. I think you're finally working through what happened to your parents."

Dusty rose from the bottom of the tank and wove his way around the plants for a minute before latching on to the side of the tank. The three friends cheered.

Then Maddy scowled as she returned to their original conversation. "Nine-lived suckerfish and going to the beach have absolutely no relation to the way my parents died."

Levi and Chrissy nodded in unison. "Exactly," he said. "That's what we've been trying to tell you for years. You've been shutting yourself off from things that used to be important to you just because your father loved them too. He's not here. You are. And so is Brody."

"For now anyway," Maddy grumbled, her heart sinking at the thought of his leaving.

"Just think," Chrissy said, "if you get over your fear of the water, you can start diving again. Kev said you used to love to dive more than just about anything in the world."

Nausea boiled just under the surface and Maddy forced a smile that felt like a transition-stage Lamaze grimace. "Not if you paid me a million dollars. Not if my own life was in danger. Not for a free Ph.D. in the field of my choice. Never. Ever. Will I dive again."

She glared at Dusty, who sucked obliviously. "Never."

"Thar she blows!"

Surprised that Ishmael had spotted a marine mammal so close to Big Jim's Pier, Brody called, "What do you see, Ishmael?"

"*Homo Sapiens Sapiens,* sir."

Curious as to why Ishmael thought it necessary to tell him there was a human being on the dock, he stood up and looked towards Big Jim's Pier.

Maddy was there, waiting for him. Waving. Smiling.

Brody's heart expanded in his chest and his smile felt like it was going to crack his whole face in half. She was on the dock. Near the water. On the beach. Waiting for him.

There was hope after all.

"Sir?" Ahab was at his elbow, tugging anxiously at his sleeve, distracting him from the lovely woman waving at him from the dock. "Dr. Davenport? Should we do something about them?"

Having been the recent butt of a particularly clever prank hatched in Smitty's deranged brain, Violet was now trying to strangle the redhead with a spare length of air hose. He was purple in the face, laughing too hard to fend her off.

Brody shrugged. "Get Ishmael and throw them both overboard to cool off."

"Sir?" Ahab's voice cracked in surprise, but his eyes lit at the prospect. "Do you mean it?"

"Yeah. Then everybody meet me up at the house. We need to decide what we're doing next."

He wanted to talk to them about staying at the Inn to work on the computer model. And he wanted Smitty's go ahead to look around Smuggler's Cove for coastal land that would support a big dock.

Though Brody was the titular leader of Dolphin Friendly, both Violet and Smitty were well-respected Ph.D.s in their own rights and would be instrumental in the startup of Brody's grand dream. He wanted their honest opinions of Smuggler's Cove. With its wealth of marine life and its mid-Cape location, he thought Smuggler's Cove might just be a perfect place to headquarter his stranding center.

And if it kept him near Maddy, that was just a bonus.

A date. They were going on a real honest-to-goodness, get-dressed-up-and-pay-for-a-candlelit-dinner-that-she-hadn't-cooked date. Brody had called from the boat and asked her out properly, and feeling brave in the aftermath of Dusty's rescue, she had thrown caution to the wind and agreed. What harm could a little dinner do?

"But I don't have a thing fit to wear," Maddy wailed. Marmalade purred, enjoying his owner's discomfort. Maddy whirled around her bedroom and pawed through the closet for the fourth time just in case a new, sexy, interesting dress was hiding in the back.

No such luck.

She touched the carving she kept on the table next to her bed, stroking a finger down the woman's cascading hair and across the dolphin's broad back. She still couldn't believe Brody had given her the carving. Couldn't believe how much she'd changed in the few weeks since.

Hopefully, he was taking her out to celebrate the news that he and his crew would be staying at least a few weeks more. Though she knew it would just make his leaving harder, she wasn't ready to say good-bye.

"Hsst! Maddy!" Levi's face appeared in her bedroom window, complete with black eye and scraped forehead from his heroic rescue effort. "Let me in."

"You couldn't use the front door?" She opened the window and helped him climb over the sill, hanging onto his belt when he leaned back out and grabbed a heavy garment bag.

"I thought it would ruin the effect."

"Effect of what?"

"Your new dress." Levi pulled a golden froth from the garment bag and held it up against her. He shook his head. "Nah. Too obvious. You need something more understated."

"Levi. What the heck's going on here?"

He chose two more dresses from the collection and discarded them both. "You told us you're going on a fantasy date with Davenport, right? Well, Chrissy and I have seen your wardrobe. We thought you needed help so I brought a few things over."

Maddy thought about arguing, then pictured the two choices she'd picked from her own closet—a rose-pink bridesmaid's dress versus an eggplant pantsuit with shoulder pads that would put Godzilla to shame. "Okay. What've you got?"

He pulled forth a sheath of silver beads. "How

about a little something I picked up for Smuggler's Cove's 'Guys and Dolls?'"

She eyed the strapless dress with longing. "You were a great doll, Levi."

"The best, babe. This here is a retro number the designer called 'The Minnow.'" He held it up and she saw how the waist nipped in and the skirt flared down like a fish's tail. "Too obvious?"

Maddy grinned. "Perfect."

There was a knock at the door and Levi called out, "We're not quite ready in here." Maddy stifled a giggle.

"I'm here to help." It was a woman's voice and Levi and Maddy looked at each other in confusion.

"Chrissy?" Maddy wondered, though it hadn't sounded like her friend's voice. She opened the door partway and looked out into the hall. "Violet?"

Stunned surprise made Maddy's grip on the door falter, and the other woman pushed her way in, dragging a duffel bag behind. They'd barely exchanged ten words in the weeks Dolphin Friendly had stayed in Smuggler's Cove, and Maddy had gotten the distinct impression that Violet couldn't stand her. Yet here she was, standing in Maddy's bedroom and nodding over Levi's choice of a dress.

"I've only got a few minutes before the others

notice that I'm gone, and it'll ruin my image if they realize I'm up here."

Wasting no time, Violet reached into the bag and pulled out a huge bulbous contraption that looked like a ray gun on steroids. She plugged in the industrial hair drier, and from the strength of the warm gale it produced, she must've set it to "tornado."

"What are you doing?" Maddy asked, though it was rapidly becoming clear what Violet was about, and that Levi fully supported the idea.

"Smitty told me I'm not allowed to say anything about your hair," the brunette said, pulling forth a terrifying collection of tubes and brushes, "but he never said I couldn't fix it."

"Still not ready?"

Brody shrugged as he retook his seat in the living room, mildly awkward in slacks and a tie when everyone else in the room was wearing cutoffs and short sleeves. "These things take time, I guess."

He didn't mention that Levi was in charge of the proceedings. Though hearing the man's voice from Maddy's bedroom had startled Brody, he figured her friends weren't any stranger than his own. In fact, he acknowledged as he watched Smitty and Violet wrangle over which gruesome videos to show the interns, the members of Dolphin Friendly were arguably weirder than the inhabitants of Smuggler's Cove.

"We haven't shown this one in years," Smitty wheedled. "We always have to watch 'Danger on the High Seas' because you think the narrator's cute. You promised last time that I could pick the next one."

"Oh, all right." Violet gave in with ill grace and plopped back down on the sofa with a bag of microwave popcorn.

There were several video collections that featured marine biology disasters caught on tape. Every once in a great while, one or two of them showed up on the networks under the heading of "Most Dangerous Careers" or "When Good Sharks Go Bad" or the like, but Dolphin Friendly used them to teach a valuable lesson to impetuous interns and summer students.

At least once in the first few weeks of breaking in new workers, Smitty and Violet would sit them down and make them watch an hour or so of "what not to do in marine biology."

Brody usually begged off these sessions since he wasn't a big fan of tabloid TV, but he recognized that the tape Smitty chose was an old one. The film was gritty and the credits were done in incredibly cheesy yellow cartoon letters. The music sounded like something straight out of a low-budget horror flick and they all groaned at the pinch-faced narrator's melodramatic introduction to "Waters of Death."

"You promise to turn this off when Maddy comes in, right?" he asked, glancing anxiously at the door every few seconds. "I really don't want her seeing even a few seconds of it. She's just starting to get more comfortable with the beach and I don't want to do anything to upset that."

"Sure, boss," Smitty agreed before beginning his lecture. He pointed to Ahab and Ishmael in turn. "Now, I want each of you to spot the moment things go bad in each scenario. Granted, this is probably ten years old and some of the equipment will be outdated, but the rules are the same. Never stop paying attention to the ocean, always triple-check your equipment, and don't get cocky." He glanced meaningfully at Brody. "And even though our boss seems to think it's okay—never, *ever* dive alone."

For the next half-hour, Smitty narrated his way through several unnecessary boating accidents, two diving mishaps and a swordboat captain catching a gaff in the leg. The interns made appropriately horrified noises and a few off-color remarks.

Brody was just getting up to check on Maddy again when a name caught his attention on the tape at the same moment that Violet gasped and Smitty breathed a quiet, "Cripes."

Maddy's face, ten years younger and shining with happiness, filled the screen. She waved and scampered to the bow of an enormous research vessel, moving awkwardly because of the diving fins on her feet and the single tank strapped between her shoulder blades.

The tape wavered and cut to a quick family portrait. Maddy stood beside a hulking young man with a silver streak in his black hair. On her other side, a man and woman who could only be her parents stood wrapped around each other, mugging for the camera. The name was repeated and Brody felt a shimmer of dread.

Marcus and Pammy Jamison. Maddy's parents. Brody felt his palms begin to sweat. The inhabitants of the cheerful little living room were paralyzed, helpless to prevent what came next.

"But Daddy, you said I could go down first this time." Young Maddy pouted when her father flicked the switch that would swing the shark cage away from the boat to dangle over the green waters of the Great Barrier Reef.

"Next time, Princess. Your mother and I are going in first today." He gestured at a dirty gray triangle that slashed through the foam near where the brother was heaving scoops of chum into the water. "We want to see the big guy up close and personal."

"Marcus? Do you want me to recheck the

winch hook where they repaired it?" The woman, an older, softer version of the landlady at the Smuggler's Inn, touched her husband's arm and he shook her off impatiently.

"No, don't bother. It's fine. Just get suited up and let's go. We're running late as it is."

There was a collective indrawing of breath. There it was. The fatal flaw. The single bad decision that precipitated disaster.

Wetsuited and strapped into her tanks, armed with an underwater camera and a spear gun that wouldn't even bring down an eight-foot-tuna, Pammy Jamison dropped lightly through the steel trap at the top of the suspended cage and locked the door behind.

The background music swelled and all hell broke loose.

With an ominous popping sound, one of the two cables suspending the shark cage over the water came loose from its davit and the cage listed drunkenly to one side. The swing of its huge bulk dragged the boat to starboard, and the brother stumbled against two huge barrels of chum.

Both barrels fell overboard, and the water immediately churned red and white with frenzied feeding behavior. The video caught Maddy's mother reaching a hand out to her daughter and husband as the second cable let go and the cage sank into the churning water.

Smitty moaned and Ishmael covered his face with both hands. The music faded so the viewers could hear a single agonized scream.

"Motherrr!" Maddy was saved from jumping into the sea only by her father, who grabbed her and flung her into her brother's arms before the older man jumped into the sea.

The screen faded mercifully to black and even the annoying narrator paused for a moment of silence before he began to read an epitaph for the husband and wife lost at sea that day.

Finally breaking free of the horror, Brody lunged across the room and slapped the TV off. He took a deep breath. And another, feeling as if he hadn't breathed in weeks. He heard a small sound and looked up, praying that she wouldn't be there.

But she was.

Chapter Ten

Maddy stood in the door wearing the most beautiful dress he had ever seen. Her hair was perfect and tears streamed down her cheeks and dripped off her chin, splashing onto the silver beads and making them shimmer like the ocean.

Her mouth was open in a silent cry of pain, and Brody's heart lurched.

He stood, spread his hands out away from his body and took two slow steps across the room, like he would approach an injured harbor seal that was just as likely to bite him as welcome his help.

"Maddy? Princess? It's okay. You're going to be all right." He crooned mindless words in a tone that usually soothed hurt creatures, and walked toward her in measured steps.

He was but a touch away when she broke free from the paralysis that held her in its grip. She looked at him, her mouth slowly closing on a gasp, and the pain in her eyes cut him to the bone.

"Maddy, I'm so sorry . . . Maddy." He held a hand to her, willing her to take it, praying that she would let him help her. Let him hold her.

But in a whirl of silver lights, she spun and was gone. Down the hall and across the porch in a flurry of beads and a clatter of heels, she fled. Brody was half a beat behind her, hard on her heels at the bottom of the porch stairs when his legs were neatly cut out from underneath him. He heard a yowl and a hiss and went down face first on the clamshell driveway.

"Meep?"

He glared at the orange tabby cat. He could swear the thing had leaped out of a rhododendron and grabbed him by the ankle, spoiling his pursuit. Heaving himself to his feet, soon joined by the rest of his crew, Brody spat a mouthful of clamshells and peered into the darkening twilight in search of a telltale flash of silver. Nothing.

"We have to find her. God, that was awful." Smitty scrubbed a trembling hand across his face and Violet nodded.

"I can't believe that was her. Poor kid." She rubbed an absent hand between Smitty's shoulders. "That must have been hell. And the brother . . ." She shivered. "Just think of what it must have done to him."

Brody nodded, the name finally adding up with the white forelock as a clue. "Darn it, I should've realized. Her brother's Tiger Jamison."

There was a moment of silence. The name was a legend in marine circles, belonging to one of the most successful, most feared shark hunters in the world. It was said there wasn't a shark Tiger Jamison wouldn't go after, but that he spent his life in pursuit of the enormous great white that killed his parents.

"Christ," Smitty breathed. "Poor Maddy."

The interns huddled miserably, and Ishmael asked in a trembling voice, "Where should we look, sir?"

Brody looked out into the still night, to the pretty homes with lamplit windows. "I have no idea."

There was so much he didn't know about her. What her favorite food was, what she had called her imaginary friend as a child, what she wanted to do with her life.

Where she would hide when she was hurt.

"Check the trail that runs along the dunes on this side," he told the interns. He gestured at Violet and Smitty, who looked like they were holding each other up. "You two work your way inland."

"Where will you be if we find her?" Ahab asked shakily.

Brody cringed, knowing what he needed to do. "At the diner. Maybe her friends'll know where she went."

It was cold. Dark.

Maddy shivered and rubbed her bare arms for warmth. She had her legs and feet pulled up inside the flared skirt of Levi's dress and she imagined that from a distance she probably looked like a misplaced disco ball.

A miserable, lost disco ball.

She rubbed her arms again and felt the ghosts of ten-year-old-bruises where her brother's fingers had pressed down to the bone while she struggled to reach their parents. She had heard rumors that an itern on board had made bootleg copies of his recordings. But she never thought she would actually stumble upon one playing in her own living room.

She could smell that day on the night air of Smuggler's Cove—the salty bite of the sea above the Great Barrier Reef, the old fish they had used to attract the sharks, the snap of exhaust from a misfiring starboard engine. The smell of marine biology.

Hugging herself, Maddy rocked.

How could she have thought it would be okay?

How stupid could she have been to think she could have a present, never mind a future, with the kind of man her father had been?

Impossible.

"I don't know where else she could have gone." Chrissy shook her head in bewilderment. "We've checked all the usual places. If she's not in the gardens behind Town Hall, then I don't have a clue."

Levi arrived, shaking his head. "Not in the gardens. Sorry, gang."

Brody almost growled in frustration. "And all of our cars are accounted for and she didn't call the cab company." That was one of the good things about a little town like Smuggler's Cove—there just weren't that many places to hide.

But by extension, it shouldn't be so hard to find her, either.

He spun and paced across Mary Jo's and back. Catching sight of a man sitting alone at the back of the diner, he stopped and said, "How about it, Ken . . . er, Kevin? Do you know where she is?"

"Why should I tell you?" The words were quiet, evenly spaced, and brought an abrupt silence to the room.

"Why?" Brody lunged for Maddy's ex-fiancé, needing to beat the heck out of something. It took Smitty and both of the interns to restrain him, which in its own way satisfied Brody's brief need for violence. He shook the others off, straightened his clothes, and shook his head. "Bad idea, sorry about that."

Kevin hadn't moved. "Why should I tell you?" he repeated as if Brody hadn't just thought to beat the information out of him.

"Because—" Brody paused. Why should Kevin tell him? The man still loved Maddy—that much was obvious. And he could give her so much of what she thought she wanted. But he couldn't possibly need Maddy as much as Brody did. "Because I love her."

Kevin scowled. "Cheap words, dolphin man. What about what she needs? If you could have seen her after her parents died, you'd think twice about making her be part of that world again. She was destroyed. It's taken her almost ten years to even think of going back to school and now what? You've brought it all crashing back. You should just go away, Davenport. She doesn't need you. She needs peace."

Brody might have taken offense but he saw that the other man was speaking from his heart, honestly trying to do what was best for the woman they both loved. So he tried to answer in kind. "With all due respect, I think you're wrong." There was a flurry of motion near the front of the diner.

He wasn't sure, but he suspected that Chrissy and Levi had just exchanged a high five.

"In what way?" Kevin asked.

"Have you ever seen the video?"

Kevin nodded. "Once, about a year after the accident. Maddy asked me to watch it with her, she thought it would help her come to terms with her parents' deaths." He shuddered. "It was awful. She didn't stop crying for a week."

"Yes, the end was awful," Brody agreed, "But only the end. Did you watch her at the beginning? I mean really watch her? She was glowing. Excited. So totally engrossed in the moment that there was nothing else for her except that boat and the people on it. She loved it. I mean really loved it."

There were a few nods around the room and Kevin scowled harder. "She doesn't love it anymore, Davenport."

"But she could. Be honest. Have you ever seen her so excited by anything as she was on that boat?"

Chrissy stepped to Kevin's side and touched his arm. "He has a point, Kev. Just think of how much trouble she's had trying to figure out what to do in school."

Brody nodded, grateful for the support. "The look in her eyes when she was all suited up and arguing with her father that she should be the first one in the water?" He wouldn't think right now about what would have happened if she hadn't been overruled. "I've seen that look before." He gestured to his crew. "We all have, in the mirror every day we get up with a job to do. When the sea's in your blood, fighting it is just going to make you crazy."

Levi took up position on Kevin's other side, and the big blond hung his head. "You're right. I know you're right, but I don't like it."

"I love her." Brody stuck out his hand as a promise. "I won't hurt her."

Kevin ignored his outstretched hand. "You already have. Now you have to fix it. But before I tell you where she is, promise me one thing?"

"What?"

"If she doesn't want to be that person again, if she doesn't want to face that part of her past, you'll let her go." Kevin's hand hovered an inch from Brody's. "Promise me that if she tells you that she doesn't want you, that she wants you and your crew to leave Smuggler's Cove, that you'll go."

Brody would have argued, but the need to get to Maddy was too strong, the need to hold her and comfort her too great. So he nodded and shook on it, though he knew it might be his loss in the end. "I promise. Where is she?"

"When she was growing up here, before her

parents died, they would leave the kids at the Inn and sail off into the sunset on another great adventure. Maddy and Tiger would follow the boat as far as they could, to those three rocks at the end of Smuggler's Point. Sometimes when she was lonely, Maddy'd go there and talk to her parents, even though they were an ocean away." Kevin shrugged. "She might be there."

"We've been looking in the wrong direction," Smitty muttered. "We never thought to check down by the water."

Kevin nodded. "Yep. I think she's gone down to the sea." He stood up, the first movement he'd made in an hour. "I'll go down with you."

But Brody stopped him with a look.

"I go alone."

The wind had picked up with the changing of the tide and Maddy was shivering in earnest now, but she barely felt the tremors.

She felt the hot breath of the Australian sun on her shoulders and the warm prickles of righteous indignation in her chest. "But Daddy, you promised!"

He'd promised that she could be first in the water today. Her brother got to go first sometimes. Her mother went first a lot. But Maddy? She never got to go first. It just wasn't fair.

"Mom?"

But her mother ducked her head and deferred to her husband as she always did. Just as she had every time Maddy asked them to stay ashore for some trivial event or another. Like her birthday. Or her high school graduation.

Sick, hot rage boiled through Maddy, chasing away the clammy chill of the night. She stood up, ignoring the silver swirl of the dress around her thighs, and grabbed a smooth rock from the sand. She heaved it with all her might into the waves that boiled around the rocky point as she pictured the man that had sired her.

"You left me! It was your fault!" She heaved another rock, unsatisfied when it sank into the sea with barely a ripple that was swamped immediately by the next swell. "You skipped your checklist and she died."

She heaved rock after rock, cursing her mother, her father, her brother, and most of all, Brody for daring her to face the demons that had been better left alone.

Yelling into the night, she threw rocks, shells, driftwood, both of her ruined shoes, anything she could get her hands on until, exhausted, she collapsed onto the low rock closest to the sea, heedless of the salt water that splashed her feet and legs, oblivious to the fact that it was the first ocean water to touch her since the day her parents died. "You promised you'd always come back."

She covered her face with her hands and felt the water creep higher on her calf.

Brody watched her from the darkness and couldn't make his feet move. It was true. Without meaning to, he had hurt her beyond measure, perhaps beyond repair. Her soft sobs tore at his heart, her huddled rocking made him despair. Then she shivered, breaking him from his trance.

"Princess, here. You're freezing."

She stiffened as he approached and batted feebly at the stranding rescue windbreaker he wrapped around her shoulders.

"I'm fine," she said, and he was surprised at how strong her voice was. "You don't need to worry about me."

He sat down next to her, close but not touching, and stretched his legs until they dangled in the water beside hers. "That's about the silliest thing I've ever heard in my life. Of course I'm worried about you."

"Don't bother. It was bound to happen sooner or later."

Brody felt the first quiver of fear. She was too composed, as if she had taken all the emotions she had to be feeling and jammed them deep down inside where they had been when Dolphin Friendly arrived. "What? The tape? Princess, if I had known, I never would have let them—"

"It wasn't the tape," she interrupted him. "And please don't call me that."

Her father had called her Princess.

"Then what are you saying?"

She laughed, a short, seal-like bark that contained no humor. "Don't be dense. It was a wake-up call. A reminder that we come from two worlds that not only don't intersect, they repel each other."

He stilled. "But Prin—uh, Maddy. You loved that world. I saw your face on the boat. You bloody well loved it."

"Loved. Past tense." She glanced over at him. "What? That's what you got out of this little adventure tonight, that I once loved being on a research boat? I have a news flash for you, Dr. Davenport. I was a kid then. I'm not a kid anymore, and I don't want that life now."

"But I thought . . ."

"Thought what? That I'd want to hop right onto *Streaker* and sail off into the sunset with you just like my mother did with my father? Think again." But her voice had grown wistful at the thought and he saw her catch her bottom lip between her teeth in the reflected moonlight.

"Maddy, I don't care if you never set foot in the water ever again." He didn't bother pointing out that both feet were currently dangling in it. "I don't care if you never want to hear about my day out on the boat, or if I never eat fish again as long as I live. I just want us to be together." He paused as the wind whistled past them loud enough to garble words. He wanted to be sure she heard these. "Maddy, I love you."

Then he strained his ears against the rising wind to hear her response, but she said nothing. Although he was sure in his heart that she loved him in return, she didn't say the words back. She was silent.

Panic started to rise on fluttery wings beating within his chest and he had to choke it down before he could speak again. "Maddy, say something. What do you want? Do you want me to stay on land? I was planning on more of that anyway, once we build the stranding center. I want to stay closer to you and maybe our kids, if you want kids, that is."

She closed her eyes and the moonlight furred the ends of her eyelashes like glitter. Her voice was rough when she said, "Brody, that's not—"

"Not what you want? Okay, what do you want? Do you want me to quit tomorrow? Then I'll—"

"Brody, stop."

He stopped.

"I was going to say that none of that is fair for either of us. I'm sure you've seen relationships like ours before. How did they work out?"

He thought of the ravaged look in Ellen's eyes when she waited for Smitty on the docks of Santa Cruz. "Not well. But I—"

"You're not going to quit. Not for me. What kind of love would that be if I asked you to give up your life?"

"But I would."

"I don't want you to."

And her meaning couldn't have been clearer if she had shouted *I don't love you* into the laughing waves.

"Well then." Brody rose to his feet, knowing if he stayed any longer he'd break down and beg.

"Your reservations end tomorrow. I think it would be best if you left then." There was a tremble in her voice, though whether from tears or cold, he couldn't tell.

"Maddy, I—"

"Go. Please," she whispered.

He went.

She waited until she couldn't hear his footsteps over the roar of the ocean and the whistle of the wind before she let her shoulders slump within his windbreaker and let her head hang down in defeat.

Did he understand that she had done the right thing? Would he ever recognize how much more painful it would have been for both of them in the long run? Or would he just hate her for turning him away, never realize how much she loved him? How her love had sent him away.

She stared out to sea until the grief turned to numbness, until the pain dulled to an ache and she realized that her feet were so cold she could barely feel them. She looked down at the water to make sure they were still attached to her ankles and saw something move.

Something gray and white with fins and teeth. Her brain yelled, *Shark! Shark! Get away, run, swim, escape!*

Maddy screamed and yanked her legs out of the water, tumbling backward off the rock in her haste to avoid certain death.

The creature recoiled in surprise, chattering noisily as it backfinned and flicked water at her with its beaklike nose. Then it spun and tailwalked a few feet before sinking back beneath the waters off Smuggler's Point.

Maddy righted herself and peeked over the top of the rock she had been sitting on. The dolphin— yes, it was a dolphin, not a great white shark— hovered just at the surface of the water with its head cocked to the side and one glistening eye staring at Maddy as if waiting for her next acrobatic move.

Gingerly, she retook her seat on the rock and dangled her feet back in the water. The dolphin, a large bottlenose with scars hatching the tough gray hide of its back, drifted closer and allowed Maddy to stroke its forehead with her toes.

"You're Brody's dolphin, aren't you?" The bottlenose warbled in answer and breathed quietly at the surface while the moonlight made crazy patterns on its dorsal fin. "The one they call Mother?"

Maddy snuggled deeper into his windbreaker and breathed in the scent that would always remind her of Brody, a silky combination of sea salt and man. She rubbed Mother's broad back with her foot and felt close to the man she had sent away.

"I had a mother once," she told Brody's dolphin. "But she's gone now."

Mother moaned softly and crowded closer to Maddy's legs, and Maddy began to talk. She told the dolphin about her mother. She told it about her father and his mistakes, and about the brother she'd barely spoken to in ten years. She told her about Brody's arrival at the Inn, about the catfish and the laundry.

She told Mother about falling in love, and about being afraid.

And as the night deepened around them and

other gray bodies gathered near, Maddy talked until, exhausted beyond measure, she fell asleep.

Throughout the night, a sleek gray guardian watched over her.

Chapter Eleven

"Please don't do anything stupid, boss." Smitty finished securing the spare Zodiac atop the pickup truck just as the sun peeked over the horizon. They had been packing since midnight in Brody's rush to be gone.

"I'm fine," he replied shortly.

"That's not what I said." Apparently seeing it was no use, Smitty scowled and desisted, for which Brody was profoundly grateful.

The last thing he wanted to do was talk.

They finished packing in silence and Brody gestured at the truck. "Take Violet and the interns with you and run this load up north to the apartments. The boat crew is getting *Streaker* ready, so when you get back we'll load the rest and get the heck out of Smuggler's Cove."

"You want us to take the second Zodiac now? I'll bet we can lash it over the SSM on the trailer."

Brody shook his head. "Leave it." He had plans for the second Zodiac.

"Being stupid isn't going to make this any better," Smitty said with a sad shake of his head. "Don't do it. Please? Talk to her again. Beg. Plead with her if you have to. But don't get yourself hurt trying to prove that you're not her father."

"I don't know what you're talking about."

"At least promise me you'll wear a full faceplate and turn on the receiver in the boat so the crew will hear you if anything goes wrong down there."

Brody's first thought was that he didn't do promises any more, but he knew that if he didn't agree, Smitty would insist on leaving one of the interns behind, and he couldn't deal with a shadow right then. "Fine," he said shortly. "I'll wear a mike."

"And make sure those two on the boat know to be listening for you."

"Whatever." Brody waved aside his friend's concern and turned his back as the Jeep and the pickup crunched down the clamshell drive and headed out of town.

Maddy's eyes opened to the rosy light of dawn. Her neck hurt, she was cold, and there was a seagull sitting three feet from her nose.

She sat up in surprise and put a quick hand to her head. It felt like it was stuffed with steel wool and she was so discombobulated it took her a moment to remember why she'd slept on the beach. Then she remembered, and gave a soft cry of pain.

The tape. Brody. She had sent him away.

Scrambling to her feet, she ignored the ruined dress that hung from her like chain mail, wrapped Brody's jacket tighter around her shoulders, and started running down the beach.

She had to find him before he left.

She had to ask him to stay.

Brody anchored the Zodiac not far from Smuggler's Point and chucked his red-and-white "diver down" flag over the side. The water was choppy and dark, with small whitecaps whipped to cresting by the wind of an incoming storm.

He'd done as Smitty had asked and switched his usual diving mask for a full faceplate that would allow him to transmit if he needed help. He'd even turned on the corresponding receiver back on *Streaker,* and yelled, "I'm going diving, radio's on," to the empty boat.

He figured that should take care of Smitty's overprotective edict.

Double-checking his wrist computer and the weights at his belt, Brody closed his eyes and fell backward into the sea. He welcomed the quick bite of the cold, for it proved that he could still feel something, and he welcomed the murk of the storm-tossed water closing in on him and cutting him off from the light, from sensation.

He could feel nothing but the heavy water, could hear nothing but the hiss of indrawn air, the rattle of expelled bubbles, and the throb of the sea around him.

Numb, he descended twenty feet, rolled to his back, crossed his arms, and drifted where the ocean would take him.

The Inn was empty. Not just of people, but of things. The guest rooms were bare of clothing and the collected debris of human habitation. Dusty was gone from the master suite. Only a towel with a rectangular imprint was left behind to mark his presence. And Brody's room was bare of his clothes, his papers, everything.

She couldn't even smell him.

"Brody?" She called his name into the emptiness though she knew it was futile. The Jeep and the pickup were both gone from the driveway.

Dolphin Friendly had left.

But no. She looked out across the land to Big Jim's Pier and saw that *Streaker* was still in her place as though waiting for her captain to tell her where to go next.

So he wasn't gone yet. There was still hope.

Maddy paused only to change from Levi's dress into jeans and a shirt, then she let herself out of the Inn and jogged to the pier. She was going to board a boat for the first time in almost ten years.

And if she had anything to say about it, she was going to stay there for the next fifty.

The drifting wasn't doing it for him. Brody just couldn't find the solace he usually got from the sea. He was itchy. Twitchy. Jumping at shadows in the slowly clearing water, and thinking too much.

His tanks bumped against something hard and he put a hand out and touched rock. His BC must have lost air, allowing him to sink a few feet closer to the bottom. Checking his wrist computer, he saw that sure enough, he was closer to the thirty-foot mark now and about halfway through his second tank.

With a few minutes left before he needed to

head for the surface, Brody let his body right it-self and perched gingerly on the rocks. They were ugly, sharp things with jagged edges, perhaps thrown down by the last passing glacier, or thrust up from the sea floor during one of the Earth's long-ago growing pains.

Sitting at the bottom of the ocean, Brody could swear he smelled flowers and sunlight.

Maddy. How could she send him away? More important, why had he left? What a fool he had been to make a clumsy declaration of love when she was in the midst of emotional upheaval, then get offended when she didn't jump right up and yell for joy.

He should have stayed with her. He should have been there for her in the dark, sat with her and talked, or just been silent if that was what she wanted. He had been wrong to leave.

But there was still time to make it right. He had sent the team away, but he hadn't left yet. He could go back to the Inn and try again. He could listen to what she had to say, then convince her that they could work it out. He was a scientist, for goodness sake—he should be able to argue the point rationally, right?

He had to. Because he wasn't leaving Maddy. If she wanted him to quit marine biology, he would. If she wanted him to move to the Midwest and raise cattle—God help him, he would.

He just had to convince her of that.

Decision made and his air just shy of the twenty-minute mark, Brody slid off the jagged rock—

And felt a searing pain in his calf.

Jerking in surprise, he flailed out wildly with a foot and felt it strike something solid and catch. *Shark!* his mind screamed, reliving the nightmarish images from the night before, and Brody Davenport, veteran of a thousand dives, came as close to panicking as he ever had in his life beneath the waves.

He thrashed wildly to escape the imagined jaws and felt his foot stick tighter and tighter yet. Then, finally a thin thread of rational thought trickled through his mind. *You're panicking. You have to calm down!* He closed his eyes and fought the rush of adrenaline, fought the feeling of claustrophobia, battered down the gibbering demons that suddenly leaped into his mind and screamed *Run! Flee! Escape!*

Counting his breaths, counting the heartbeats that thundered in his ears, Brody slowly mastered his own body. Then he took stock of the situation.

The pain in his leg throbbed with every beat of his heart, and when he looked down he could just make out a tear in his wetsuit at the back of his thigh. Blood seeped from the rent, puffing dark in the swirling water.

Not life-threatening. Easy to treat on *Streaker.*

Then he cast his attention lower, to the foot that he couldn't quite move and his guts turned to water. His fin was mangled beyond repair, jammed between two fanglike rocks. And his foot was wedged with the strap from the flipper pulling it one way and the rough stone surface jamming it the other.

He was stuck.

"Hello?" Maddy stepped onto *Streaker*'s deck, feeling as if there ought to be a live band playing to celebrate her return to the sea. But there was no band. In fact, the boat seemed deserted.

"Is anyone here?" No answer. It seemed odd that *Streaker* should be alone as though she too had been left behind in Dolphin Friendly's exodus.

Feeling like an intrepid adventurer exploring an uncharted rainforest, Maddy picked her way through the boat, finding things that were at once familiar and unfamiliar. Technology had exploded in the years since she had last crewed for her father on his beloved *Poseidon's Reach,* and even the diving equipment she found neatly arranged in lockers belowdecks looked as if it had been designed by aliens.

In the engine room she found a note pinned to the starboard engine that read *Plugs are bad, we've gone to get fresh. We'll get the radio hand-set fixed while we're out. Back soon.* Well, that explained the absence of even the boat crew.

Maddy smiled. She was on a boat again and it wasn't horrible. She didn't peer around each corner, fearful of seeing her father's face or hearing her mother's futile banging at the bars of the sinking shark cage.

She was alone here. No ghosts haunted her. She was aboard Brody's boat, and the future stretched before them like a gilded road. But he didn't know that yet.

"Where are you, love?"

And as if in answer to her question, a radio spluttered to life in the wheelhouse.

Brody paused and wet his lips. He stared at his wrist computer as if wishing it so would create a few pounds more air.

He had ten minutes, give or take a couple.

The water had cleared as the waves had subsided slightly, and he could see the surface twenty-five feet above his head. It seemed like a mile.

Gritting his teeth, he attacked his dive fin once again with his hands, trying to rip it apart with brute strength borne of terror. His dive knife would have helped, but it was packed with the rest of his luggage.

Check and double-check, his mind mocked.

At least the bleeding had stopped, no longer a glowing beacon to nearby predators. He hoped.

Breath rattled in his lungs as he tugged again and again at his foot, and for the first time in his life he understood how a trapped animal could gnaw its own paw off to escape.

Maddy! I'm so sorry.

His only consolation was that he hadn't promised her he'd come home safe that evening. At least he wouldn't break that promise.

The thought was little comfort.

With a last futile tug at his leg, which succeeded only in jamming it tighter between the rocks, Brody toggled his radio to send and called for help again.

As the warning light on his wrist computer flashed from yellow to red, signaling that he was direly low on air, Brody wondered whether anyone was even listening.

He began, "Mayday, mayday—" and broke off as a gray-and-white shape undulated slowly above him. It paused, then circled back.

It wasn't one of the dolphins.

As Maddy opened the door to the wheelhouse, the small radio next to the fish finder hissed and popped like overheated stir-fry. She wouldn't have bothered to follow the sound, except that it was the only sign of life on the boat and she was starting to feel a little creeped out by the silence.

Then there were words.

"Mayday, mayday . . ." More static, but Maddy felt the blood in her veins turn to ice and her stomach swirl like a tornado. That had sounded like Brody's voice. But it couldn't be, could it? He was gone with the others. They'd left hours ago.

Then she remembered that his diving equipment had been missing from his locker. The fool hadn't gone down without a partner, had he?

The static again resolved itself into broken words. ". . . Davenport. I'm stuck and . . . minutes of air left. My leg is cut and . . . shark."

"Brody!" She scrambled furiously for a way to respond, a way to radio him back. How badly was he hurt? How many minutes of air did he have left? And the shark. Dear God. He was bleeding and there was a shark nearby.

Then she remembered the note in the engine room. They had taken the handset to be fixed. She couldn't radio him back. Couldn't radio the coast-guard.

There was another series of hissing pops, then a single sentence, very clear. "Tell Maddy that I'm sorry and I love her. End transmission."

"No! Not the end. I won't let it be!"

Think, Maddy. Think. The cell phone. She

grabbed it, dialed 911 and blurted out a Coast Guard emergency before the operator could get a word in edgewise.

"Where is he? In the water somewhere. I don't know." But she grabbed the binoculars that hung over the captain's chair and scanned the cove. She caught a flash of red and white, squinted until she could make out the Zodiac anchored nearby. "Wait, there he is. Just off Smuggler's Point. Come quickly." And she disconnected before the woman could stammer a reply.

Too late. They'd be too late.

Without stopping to think, Maddy tore down the stairs and bolted into the locker room. She ran to the cubby marked "Violet" and grabbed swim fins, a mask, a harness and tank that thankfully showed an almost full load of compressed air, a BC and weight belt. She jammed the small stuff into a duffel bag she found in Smitty's locker and hoisted it onto her shoulder.

And she ran for the small motorboat Big Jim kept at the pier for his nieces and nephews to take fishing.

The blinking red light had become Brody's friend. Not only did it tell him he had run out of air, it kept time with his heart and gave him something to focus on other than the shark that was circling him slowly. It wasn't much of a shark, really. Just a medium-sized sand shark. They weren't killers so much as scavengers and under normal circumstances, Brody would've shooed it away and gone on with his business.

But right now, his business was breathing, which was getting harder by the minute.

The shark swam by. It was beautiful in a way, and Brody envied it the slit-like gills that pulled oxygen out of the salt water as the creature swam. He could reach out and touch it if he chose to. It was that close. But he knew its skin would be rough and harsh, not like the rubbery dolphins he loved so much.

Mother, where are you? he thought.

He wasn't sure if he was calling his dolphin friend or the woman who had raised him on a dusty cattle farm, but as his vision grayed with lack of oxygen, he suddenly smelled fresh flowers and sunlight.

Jerking convulsively in the direction of that sunlight, Brody thought he felt the swim fin finally give way and release his foot, but it was too late. As the weight belt pulled him to the sea floor and the shark undulated down to investigate, Brody's last thought echoed in his mind.

Maddy, I'm so sorry.

She didn't start shaking until she had the motorboat anchored next to the Zodiac and had managed to put all of Violet's equipment in approximately the right places, alien technology and all. Once the gear was all on, feeling both familiar and strange, Maddy could do nothing more than stand and stare down into the greasy gray water.

I can't do this.

"I have to," she said, and clamped Violet's regulator between her teeth and ignored the faint taste of stale lipstick and grape bubblegum.

As she swung her finned feet over the side, she saw a glint of metal beneath the aft seat and grabbed for it, knowing that Big Jim kept a barbed gaff in his boat for landing big fish.

It would do in a pinch as a shark deterrent.

"Brody!" Mumbling his name around the regulator and screaming it in her head, Maddy spun and tumbled backward into the sea, screaming again as the water closed over her and the cold lashed her with icy flails as she tumbled down and down again.

She stopped breathing. She panicked. Every muscle in her body shut down, seized up and jerked uncontrollably. Tears streamed down her cheeks inside her facemask and if she could have clawed her way back up to the surface and onto the boat, she would have done it without a second thought. But the weights were too heavy, the buoyancy vest too strange and she sank like a stone.

Pressure rattled crazily in her brain and she popped her ears, equalizing them before they ruptured.

And then she was on the bottom, about thirty feet down. Her landing kicked up a cloud of silt and she couldn't see. There might be a shark inches from her and she wouldn't know.

She crouched and swiped the gaff in front of her, swirling up more sediment and hitting nothing. *Stop it,* she ordered. *Act rationally. Fix your buoyancy and move away from the murky water.*

Thus coached, she adjusted her BC to counteract Violet's heavy weight belt until she was hovering a few feet above the silty cloud. Sight limited to the patch afforded to her by the goggles, she fanned her fins and turned her body in a slow arc while breathing in slow, regular gulps.

She saw sand. She saw an old New York license plate. She saw green water and a glimmer of light from the surface, not too far above. She continued turning.

And saw him.

He drifted limply and there was the barest trickle of bubbles escaping from his regulator. There was a six-inch tear in the neoprene covering his right thigh. And there was a medium-sized shark tugging at his one remaining swim fin.

Sand shark, her brain supplied, and though it had been years since she'd swum with them, Maddy felt some of her fear ebb. Ignoring the creature, she finned over to Brody, yanked his full faceplate off, and jammed Violet's auxiliary regulator into his mouth. The backup regulator ran off the tanks on Maddy's back and would provide him enough air to stay alive while they swam to the surface.

Breathe, she ordered the motionless wetsuited figure. *Breathe!*

There was a gray blur at the periphery of her vision, a bigger, faster blur than the sand shark. Maddy jerked and spun to meet the new threat, her heart pounding as hard as it had when she first went into the water.

But it wasn't the yellow-gray torpedo of another, more deadly shark. These gray skins were rubbery and the noses long and the mouths that turned up in laughing smiles contained a less ferocious set of teeth.

The dolphins had arrived, drawn by the noise or the blood, or by the otherworldly empathy of the sea, and they clicked sharply, excitedly when a thin stream of bubbles erupted from the backup regulator and Brody's legs kicked feebly.

Thank God.

It wasn't until he'd sucked in a few life-giving breaths and his eyes had opened, squinting into the stinging salt, that Maddy began to shake. She'd been braver than she ever thought possible, but now that it was over she wanted nothing more than to be back on dry land. Safety.

She gestured toward the surface above, where the silhouettes of the Zodiac and the powerboat hovered side by side, and Brody nodded. He touched her cheek with a fingertip, then repeated her gesture.

The younger dolphins were entertaining themselves by pestering the sand shark, but Mother swam slowly beside the humans as they kicked for the surface, keeping pace with them as though they were the weakest of dolphin calves.

When they broke free into the air, Mother was right beside them, whistling excitedly when she saw the Coast Guard cutter bearing down on them with a bow wave that looked perfect for surfing. Before she left, she touched each of the humans with her rostrum as if to say, "Stay well," then she was gone with a puff of breath and a flick of her powerful flukes.

Brody yanked the octopus from his mouth and yelled, "Thank you, Mother! And stay away from the beaches for a while, you hear?"

There was a cheer from the cutter as it drifted to a stop nearby and Maddy spat out her regulator and waved her goggles over her head in thanks as they dropped a rope ladder over the side. Then she turned to Brody.

And felt suddenly shy.

"If—"

"I—" They started to speak simultaneously, then broke off with identical laughs. A swell shifted under them and Maddy dipped her head back into the brine. A thousand goosebumps marched their way up and down her arms and legs but she didn't care. She was alive. And in love. "I can't wait to get back on land. I've never been so scared before in all my life." She glanced at Brody. "What were you going to say?"

His gray green eyes were silty with love, murky with pain. "You were wonderful. I can't believe you went down after me." He glanced up at the waving Coast Guardsmen and back at Maddy. "And I was stupid to leave you last night. I love you, Maddy. If you marry me, I promise I'll never ask you to go near the water again."

She cocked her head. "Never?" Her heart picked up its beat when she imagined the long days and nights ahead of them. He loved her. It was going to be okay. The ocean shifted against her skin, and it felt like coming home. "How about a different promise?"

Brody nodded. "Anything."

"I'll marry you if you promise not to dive alone anymore."

He cocked his head and looked deep into her eyes, trying to decide if she was saying what he thought she was saying. "On one condition."

"Conditions already?" But she smiled. "What condition?"

"That you think about being my diving partner now and again." His eyes grew greener, his lips drew closer. "There's so much I want to show you, love."

She smiled and nodded. "It's a deal, love." She sealed it with a kiss that went on.

And on.

Epilogue

"Are the new interns here yet?"

Smitty rolled his eyes at Violet, who bit back a grin. "Not yet, boss. Just like they weren't here five minutes ago when I told you the launch was still twenty minutes away."

Streaker swayed gently in the light chop off St. John and from inside the sonar room, the fish finder beeped as it picked up a large contact. Grateful for some sort of activity to take his mind off the arrival of the new interns, Brody checked it out.

A big school of something. Cod probably. Boring. But while he readjusted the settings and took a moment to check the sonar, he admired the glint

180

of the green from the weather radar on the gold of his wedding ring.

Designed by Chrissy's husband, Michael, the ring was a wide band with the etched figure of a long-haired woman astride a laughing dolphin.

"Brody, they're here!"

He paused briefly to check his appearance in the reflection of a diving mask. It had only been a week since they'd seen each other last, but it had been the longest seven days of his life.

"Brody!"

He ran to the deck and watched the three newest members of Dolphin Friendly leap from the launch onto *Streaker*'s bow. He had a whole speech he gave every time new interns joined the boat, and had planned to give it that day as well. It was a zippy ten-minute talk full of cautions and rules interspersed with enough anecdotes to entertain the trio of interns, all third-year students from the UCSC marine sciences program.

But instead he felt a big, goofy grin split his face and he ran to the first intern he saw and grabbed her in a big hug, picked her up off her feet, and swung her around and around in dizzying circles while he kissed her face, her throat, that little spot behind her ear, anything he could reach.

"You're here!"

So much for the new intern speech, but Brody didn't care. She was here. Maddy was on *Streaker* with him and she was there to stay.

She framed his face with her hands and kissed him softly, and said, "Yep. I'm here, but only on one condition."

Brody heard a chuckle from behind him, and Violet whispered, "Conditions already? It's going to be a long trip back to the temporary headquarters of the Smuggler's Cove Stranding Center, folks."

"What condition?"

Maddy smiled and linked her hands behind his neck and whispered, "No videos."

"No videos," he agreed, and set her down on the deck before introducing himself to the other interns.

"Anchors up?" asked Smitty and Brody shook his head.

"Nah, let's wait an hour or so." He held a hand out to Maddy and gloried when he felt her fingers grasp his own.

"I'm going diving with my wife."

He turned to her and pulled her close, whispering. "There're dolphins down there I want you to meet."

And she did.